HURRICANE SEASON

MJ CORKERN

HURRICANE SEASON. Copyright © 2020 by M.J. Corkern
ISBN: 978-0-578-76144-2

CONTENTS

INTRODUCTION

I wasn't going to include this because I am notorious for skipping introductions, but there are some things you need to understand so that you can fully appreciate this story.

I'm not sure how to introduce you to the story you're about to read. I didn't think I'd write about it, because I don't necessarily want to attract attention to myself. I'm really just an ordinary girl who took a leap of faith, not knowing where I'd land. This story isn't just my own; I share it for anyone who has lived a life similar to mine. I need those people to know they're not alone.

I was born in the early 1990's and grew up enveloped in Evangelical Christianity, specifically, a non-denominational, charismatic sect of the religion. Church was my entire life. I sang in the children's choir, got baptized, spoke in tongues and had people "lay hands" on me for healing. I was neck-deep in what I now see as a cultish belief system.

From as long as I can remember, I was taught and shown

that my body wasn't mine, my heart was wicked, and that my thoughts were to be "taken captive under Christ" before they could be trusted. It was all-consuming.

When I got married, I had already done a lot of work to change my way of thinking and to unlearn some of the things I had been indoctrinated to believe. I no longer attended church regularly, I switched political affiliations, and I had moved an hour or so away from my town and into a city. I would go out drinking with friends, and never once tried to evangelize them like I would have back in my church days. Even though I continued to pray and believe, I was living a "normal" life, one where church wasn't my entire world as it had once been.

But something was still amiss. There was still one hurdle I couldn't seem to get past, no matter how hard I tried: purity doctrine.

Despite my inner objections, I couldn't shake the belief that sex before marriage was a not only a sin, but a big sin, one that could ruin a person's life. This doctrine told me that once I was married, it was my obligation to give my husband sex, and if I didn't, he could cheat on me and it would be my fault because men *need* sex. None of it felt right, especially after I moved to Austin and met people who didn't think twice about hooking up. I discovered that not every woman struggled to remain "pure" or felt shame for even thinking about sex.

When I stepped away from all that is where this story begins. I had been doing internal work for a few years. I'm sharing the part of my story where it finally gets good--or bad, depending on how you see things.

I encourage you to sit back, relax, and enjoy the ride of my life.

Chapter One

MARRIAGE VACATION

"ARE YOU SURE THIS IS THE RIGHT THING TO DO, THEO?" I asked. Uncertainty plagued my mind, even though we'd been over this plan again and again.

I had less than twenty minutes before I had to leave for the airport and there I was, half dressed and still struggling to force my crumpled jeans into my bag. Theo hugged me from behind, reaching his arms around me and gently removing the pants from my grip, kissing me softly on my shoulder. My tense body softened and melted into his.

"I'm sure," he told me confidently as he placed my favorite jeans into my suitcase.

"Are you gonna..." Paralyzed by insecurity, I paused, unable to finish my question.

"What, fuck someone else?" Theo quipped.

I nodded my head and looked away, not wanting to hear the answer, though I already knew.

"If I want to." Theo answered directly. He continued, "That's what we agreed, I will do whatever I want to, but I'm not seeking it. I had a fulfilling sex life before I met you. I know what sex is, Hillary. You don't."

His words struck a nerve. He was right, and I hated it. All I could do was resume packing while he lounged across the bed--our bed. We had been through so much together. Things were easier before we got married, when sex wasn't part of the equation. Now, having been married less than two years, sex had us on the brink of divorce. This was our last shot. We'd tried everything else. We had read all the books on marriage we could find, gone to couples counseling, even attended a weekend long marriage seminar my old church hosted, but our problems weren't exactly common, which rendered our efforts futile.

With little time to spare, I finished packing. As I looked around my bedroom knowing it would be the last time I set foot there for a long time, a wave of grief washed over me. I surveyed the pictures that hung on the wall, taking a moment to admire the photo of our very first date. I noticed the books that lined our shelves; some Christian, some self-help, some steamy romance novels. I quickly shoved the erotic fantasy series into my purse. Plagued by doubt, I questioned our decision. What was I doing? Would this marriage vacation help me? Help us? I didn't know, but what else could we do? Divorce was our next step, which would bring more shame and judgement than I was ready to handle. Of course, I was also afraid of the ridicule I would face if my hometown community found out my husband and I were opening our marriage and spending six months apart. According to the Evangelical culture in which I grew up, sex outside of marriage was an egregious offense.

I joined Theo on the bed, took his hands in mine and asked another question I didn't want to hear the answer to.

"What if this breaks us?" Tears tried to escape my eyes. I didn't know if we would make it through six months of living separately. All I knew was that I wanted to change and grow during my time away. I wanted to become the person I was meant to be.

"This will only break us if you let it," he said, wrapping his arms around me. "I am in this. One hundred percent." I leaned into his chest, soaking in every last second we had together before I left.

I appreciated his reassurance. There was a time when Theo was ready to give up on us. He was tired of trying; tired of doing the same things over and over again hoping for different results. At least now, we were trying something different. Drastically different.

After a deep, long exhale, I sighed, "I love you so much."

"I know. I love you so much, too." Theo replied. He did. Theo really loved me, but I worried this move would cause our already fragile marriage to crumble.

The alert on my phone interrupted our embrace.

"Six months isn't that long," I told him, neither of us loosening our grip on the other. We knew this was our best bet, but we were both reluctant to let go. Me, more than him. "I'll be back before we know it." I said, trying to assure myself. The alert went off again.

"My driver is outside," I told him, pulling away from the hug. Theo grabbed my suitcase, I threw my carry-on over my shoulder, and we walked out to the car.

"You aren't doing anything wrong, Hillary. Don't beat your-self up. You've spent most of your life condemning yourself for everything you do, everything you don't do. Even your thought life is under scrutiny. If you don't strip yourself of all that, you won't grow. I won't leave you unless you want me to. Our relationship is strong enough to survive a six month break."

Theo's confidence in me and in us gave me the courage to walk out the door, though not without trepidation. The thought of being able to do whatever or whoever I wanted, whenever I wanted both thrilled and terrified me. No one would be there to judge or shame me. My husband supported me, and since it's no one's business but his who, or what, I did, no one else had to know. But I'd know. Could I handle it?

En route to the airport, my mind wandered as I tried to avoid small talk with my overly chatty driver. How did I get here? What would my parents think? What about our pastor? How would our friends react to this? Does anyone else who grew up like me suffer the way I do? Will this ruin my marriage? My life? Is this a mistake? Am I a whore?

Considering my Evangelical upbringing, I never imagined this would be my life at twenty- eight. I thought I would have children, that I would be going to bed with Theo every night for the rest of our lives. I thought I would be farther along in my writing career. Like they say, we plan and God laughs. God probably wasn't laughing now. When I heard the Gate Agent over the speaker saying, "We are now boarding flight 1020 to New Orleans," I was tempted to grab my bag and run out of the airport, but I didn't. I had made a commitment to myself. To Theo. How crazy is it that I committed to sleeping with other people in order to help save my marriage? Crazy enough for me to create a writing assignment as a cover story so no one knew why I was really going to New Orleans.

I would be back sometime in December with a piece about life in Post-Katrina New Orleans during hurricane season. If nothing else came of the trip, I would at least have an article that would sell for enough to cover some of my expenses living in, as the locals call it, NOLA.

Before we settled on a location, Theo and I did a ton of research. I needed to go somewhere with a good nightlife and rich culture. I was searching for a city with a story to be told. Vegas was too cliché. That's where everyone would go to get laid. We didn't want to take on the expense of big cities like Los Angeles or New York. I almost ended up in Chicago, but being a Texas girl, I really wanted to stay in an area with sweet tea, fried chicken, and southern hospitality.

I had never been to N'awlins before. If I was going to live like a local, I wanted to act like a local, so I had plenty of homework to do. The first thing I learned is that locals never call it N'awlins. It's New Or-lens or NOLA. Anything else is reserved for tourists or people who have only seen the city portrayed in movies. I also learned it's a laid back town, and there is a thing called "New Orleans time" which is almost like island time, but not exactly. Folks in the social media group I'd joined assured me I would understand New Orleans time once I got there.

I spent most of the plane ride wavering between looking forward to my adventure and making myself sick with self-doubt. I wasn't exactly excited about having casual sex, but I wasn't repulsed by the idea either. After a short flight I landed in New Orleans on a sunny May afternoon, not quite sure what I was getting myself into.

Looking back, I can see that things played out exactly the way they needed to in order to get me to a place where I could share my story. It has been almost two years since my plane touched down at Louis Armstrong International Airport in New Orleans, where I embarked on a journey nothing could have prepared me for, yet one I was destined to take.

Chapter Two

BOLD GIRL

"THIS IS MY FIRST TIME HERE!" I NERVOUSLY EXCLAIMED TO MY cab driver. Now I was the one being chatty. The drive from the airport to my rental was only twenty minutes. I was glad the town seemed to be situated in such a way to justify my decision to skip getting a car. I found myself wondering why I had spent all my life in a neighboring state and never visited New Orleans? Probably because of its reputation of being a city of hedonism and decadence, two things my church hated. I never expected to find myself there, intentionally diving headfirst into debauchery. I spent the rest of the ride trying to convince myself I was strong and could handle whatever was to come.

I arrived at my new home: an off-white shotgun double with maroon trim in an area of New Orleans a few miles from the French Quarter called Bayou St. John, which was very much *not* a bayou. A "shotgun" is an elevated rectangular home without hallways or side rooms. I stepped from the front porch directly into the living room, which led to the bedroom, then finally the kitchen, which was located at the back of the house.

In those first moments I was in a daze, unable to fully process what was happening. In this alternate reality, I was no longer Theo's wife; I was a single woman in a new city. For the next six months, this would be *my* shotgun double with *my* front porch swing. "This is *my* bed," I thought, as I ran my fingers across the dark wooden headboard. I took the floral sheets between my fingers, surprised to find they were as stiff as cardboard. If I was going to invite someone back here, I would have to find something more suitable for my bed. I wondered if I would have the guts to invite someone into my new bed. I spent my first several days gathering my thoughts, stocking the fridge, and learning how to pronounce Tchoupitoulas.

Tired of looking at blank walls and sleeping on rough sheets, I made my way Uptown to Magazine Street in hopes of scoring some local art, and maybe some bedding that wouldn't deter potential suitors. My attempts at navigating public transport could be summed up as disastrous. I spent most of the afternoon going from bus stop to bus stop, waiting at one place for well over an hour before I used a ride-sharing app to get me the rest of the way. I'd been living in New Orleans for less than seven days and I was already reconsidering my decision to go without a car.

As I popped in and out of one local art shop after another, I pondered my plan. If I was there to have sex with people, I might as well get started. In the boutique where I found my new bedding, I noticed the attendant, Will, was kind of cute in a non-threatening way. He looked to be about 24 years old--a little young for me, but I was here to experiment, wasn't I? I was freshly showered, my legs shaved and bikini area groomed. I was on birth control and had condoms in my purse. I decided to go ahead and rip the band aid off.

I took a deep breath and mustered all the courage I could find as I leaned over the counter and said, "I'm buying these new sheets so I can have sex with someone on them. Any chance you want to be that someone?" His eyes widened as my brazen words shocked him out of his monotonous workday trance.

"I... I'm at work another 30 minutes," he replied, trying to figure out if I was serious. I bit my lower lip and held his gaze in a way that I hoped was seductive, my eyes and body language telling him I meant every word. "I'm in no rush," I replied. "I'll be at the coffee shop next door. Come find me when you're done." The voice coming out of my mouth was filled with so much confidence I hardly recognized it as my own.

I was never a bold girl; that's not what a "Godly" man would have wanted. Growing up in the Evangelical church I was taught to be submissive, demur; helpless even. No one said these things to me directly, of course, but the message was loud and clear. Strong women stayed single and "Proverbs 31 women" married successful Christian men. We were instructed that if we could "wait on the Lord" and pray for our future spouse, we'd be rewarded with a blessed, happy marriage. God would help us remain pure as we waited on His perfect timing. I found it strange that in my youth group, the so-called perfect timing was typically the dawn of adulthood. Some of the people from my church married as young as 18 and 19 years old.

"Hey... Ashley, is it?" A voice came from behind me. I turned to see Will strolling up with a nervous glee I had never seen on a grown man before. He reminded me of a child about to taste candy for the first time. I hadn't told him my name, but I figured I'd just go with Ashley.

"Yeah! Hey!" I said playfully. Will grinned. "So... are you ready?"

I was ready in the practical sense, but emotionally? My fears of disobeying God bubbled to the surface. I knew if this trip was going to be worth anything, I would have to physically experience sex with other people. I needed to learn why I was so uncomfortable with my body and my desires. I couldn't do it with Theo; maybe I could with Will. He was cute, kind, and consenting. There was no reason not to sleep with him except for my own deep-rooted fears of sex and sexuality.

After a momentary pause, I replied, "I am. Can we take your car? I'm new in town, and I didn't realize a car was a must in this city."

"Sure. And yeah, you won't get too far without a car here."

"I can tell. I tried taking the bus and..." I started to tell him my ordeal trying to get to Magazine Street earlier that day.

"Wait, we have a bus system?" He interrupted, with a surprised look on his face. "I had no idea."

"You're cute," I told him giggling and reaching out to rub his shoulder. I started to feel a little excitement about fooling around. The idea of having sex with a stranger was beginning to entice me.

On the drive to my shotgun double, I told Will all about my life and my marriage vacation experiment. Since he didn't know my real name or where I was from, I figured he was safe. Plus, he was very into this whole thing. "I'm on a quest to save my marriage by exploring my sexuality. I want to overcome the shame inflicted upon me as a young girl growing up in Evangelical Christianity during the height of what is known as the purity movement, so, basically, I need to have a lot of sex," I explained. Will nodded as he pressed the gas pedal harder, his body unconsciously signaling his arousal at my strange yet alluring disclosure.

Before I knew it, we were back at my place having drinks. Unsure of how to proceed, I asked him if he wanted to make out. As things became more heated between us, he fumbled with my bra and almost tripped as he removed his pants.

Being with someone else for the first time was nothing like I imagined. I thought we would be overcome with passion, barely able to get each other's clothes off before we started going at it. I was terribly mistaken; sex with Will was awkward and clumsy. Though I tried to appear cool and comfortable, my body was tense. I was too in my head; I didn't even finish. Worse still, even though I knew Theo and I were on the same page, it felt like I was cheating.

It wasn't a really good experience, but the band aid had been successfully ripped off. After he left, a sense of relief came over me, but was quickly followed by crushing guilt. I spent the rest of the night sobbing in a ball on my shower floor, hoping somehow the water could wash away my impurity. I sat there for what seemed like hours, water beating on my face and tears pouring out of my eyes. I thought about when I was eleven years old and I learned that my purity wasn't about my good heart or compassion for others, but instead directly tied to my virginity. I wasn't pressured to do anything to improve my community or help the less fortunate, instead I was sternly warned to remain an untarnished virgin.

When I was a little girl, I saw myself as pure. My heart was good. I loved people and didn't think too much of myself. In fact, I rarely thought of myself at all. These days, all I did was think of myself. Deconstructing my religion had taken over my life the last few years. I was finally taking active steps to release the burden placed on me by the church. The God I knew as a young girl, the God of love and grace, who cared for the poor and the broken, had been replaced during my adolescence by a new God who only seemed to care about who we were having sex with, thinking about having sex with, or tempting into sex. Of course, the tempting was strictly attributed to us girls; we were the temptresses. This new God would really hate it if we gave in to our biological urges. Urges that were supposedly part of His design.

Shortly after I turned eleven, I attended an Evangelical coming-of-age tradition known as a Purity Ball. It was an exciting day. My mom gave me a white flowy dress with sequins along the neckline, curled my hair, and even let me put on shiny lip gloss. There was an impromptu photoshoot in the backyard. I basked in the special attention from my parents. My dad bought me a bouquet of flowers, opened the car door for me. This was intended to demonstrate how a man should treat a woman.

We arrived at the ball and my excitement quickly turned to fear and embarrassment when I learned I was expected to publicly dedicate myself to God as someone who would remain pure until marriage. I stuttered into the microphone, my prepubescent high pitched voice promising my dad and God that I wouldn't engage in sexual intercourse until I was married. I carefully scrawled my messy signature on a purity pledge certificate and placed a white rose, which was supposed to symbolize purity, at the foot of a giant wooden cross. Nothing about the experience made sense to me. As I looked around the room, everyone else seemed to be having such a great time, so I thought something was wrong with me. I spent the rest of the night numbing my shame at the dessert bar.

After the ball, the church leaders took their purity gospel teachings to the next level. I can still hear the words they told us over and over:

"Your body is a temple."

"Sexual sin is the worst sin because it's a sin against your own body."

"You don't want to lead boys into temptation."

"Satan is the author of temptation."

"Eve ate the apple."

"God caused childbirth to be painful as a punishment for Eve's sin."

These almost exclusively male leaders spent countless hours spewing nonsense claiming we, as girls, were responsible for boys' sexual purity and pretty much all the sexual sin in the world. If they had spent half as much time teaching us how to care for the environment, we might not be in the middle of a global warming crisis right now. Why did sex matter above all else? We didn't have "Philanthropic Balls" or "Compassion Balls" but we didn't miss a Purity

Ball. My virginity got a public pledge; my commitment to the "least of these" did not. Apparently my hunger and thirst for righteousness was not as important as my intact hymen.

Even after waiting until marriage, I was plagued with guilt over sex. Years of conditioning were stripped away on that shower floor, bringing both pain and healing.

I awoke the next morning wondering how Theo would respond to me having sex with someone else. We had tried addressing this issue between ourselves and with various therapists only to be left with no other choice but for me to explore my sexuality. My biggest struggle was feeling unclean; impure. Like a seductress. I didn't truly believe I had anything to feel bad about, but I couldn't get past the indoctrination that told me I *should* feel bad. How could sex be worse than cutting funding for free lunch at impoverished schools? I came to the conclusion that the Jesus of the Bible was far more concerned about greed and self-righteousness than extramarital sex.

Chapter Three

ABORT MISSION

"Can I get an Iced Mocha?" I asked Angelique, the barista at my favorite newfound coffee shop in the city.

Near the end of June, I had an uncomfortable first (and only) meeting for my article. Although it originated as a cover story for my time in New Orleans, I was excited to work on this Katrina project. I sat down with Beverly, a woman who lived near the Baptist Seminary in eastern New Orleans, at a downtown coffee shop late Saturday afternoon. As we sipped our lattes, she told me her story of loss and recovery. She had a unique perspective which troubled me. In describing the aftermath of a large portion of the area near the seminary being flooded, including her home, she sat her mug down, leaned over the table toward me, and confessed in a hushed tone, "I don't know why so many church leaders said that storm was God's punishment on New Orleans. If that were the case, why did the seminary get hit so hard but not the French Quarter?" I wondered how she could be so sure the school was above reproach, and why the French Quarter I had quickly grown fond of should have faced such dire consequences. If the French Quarter had flooded like the seminary did, it would only further erode the city's economy, causing the poorest in the area to suffer. While Beverly was kind to me, she was blissfully unaware of her privilege as a wealthy white Christian who was fortunate enough to receive part of a multi-million-dollar donation to help rebuild her home and replace her possessions. She did not seem to give one thought to those around her who had endured a fate far worse than she. I wanted to include her story, but I wasn't sure I could give her a platform.

I put away my notes, sighing at what appeared to be a wasted interview, and stepped out to the humid air to clear my head with a stroll around the French Quarter--the same French Quarter Beverly would have destroyed during Katrina if she were God. I was frustrated with that interview, knowing it was probably a waste of time, and frustrated that my only sexual encounter so far had been with the eager but lackluster Will. I was beginning to second-guess everything. I texted Theo, telling him I missed him. He didn't respond. It was less than a month into my trip and I'd already broken our no contact rule. I was both angry and grateful that he ignored me.

As the evening faded into night, I was ready to head home, feeling defeated. One of the things I came to love about New Orleans is you never know when there's going to be a parade. You could be walking out of a meeting one minute and find yourself smack dab in the middle of a brass band parade, known as a "second line", the next. As I rounded the corner of Royal St. I was suddenly swept up into a second line for a newly married couple. The bride and groom were wielding umbrellas, black for him and white for her, and the guests trailing behind shook their lavender handkerchiefs as they marched along the impromptu route. I was dancing to the music from the sidewalk when out of the corner of my eye, I caught a glimpse of the wedding photographer. My heart stopped. My mind raced. Was that really him?

"Jacob!" I exclaimed as we locked eyes, surprise and recognition flashing across my high school boyfriend's face as he grinned at me.

"Hillary!" He pulled me into a hug and my knees weakened.

"What are you doing in NOLA?" He asked incredulously.

"I'm here on an assignment, what about you?" I told him, dying to know how long he'd be in town.

"I live here now," he casually replied. I went into an internal frenzy. Jacob was here, living in the city where I was free to do whatever I wanted. And I had been wanting to do Jacob since high school.

"WHAT?" I said, unable to hide my utter shock. "Well, I'll be here for the next six months covering Hurricane Season," I blurted out. I was ecstatic at the idea of reconnecting with Jacob. He could relate to me in a way Theo never could; he understood first-hand what it was like to grow up in a fundamentalist religion.

"Oh shoot! I've gotta run; I'm losing the bride and groom," Jacob said, gripping his camera and preparing to run off. "Look me up online!" He yelled, his words fading as he blended into the crowd of wedding guests, party goers, and a 4-piece brass band.

As I reflected on what had just happened, I thought it might be best to let Jacob go and forget I'd ever run into him. What if my feelings for him came back? I was already weak in the knees just from seeing him for a second. I didn't know if I could handle this. I wanted to sleep with him so badly I could feel it in my teeth.

My encounter with Jacob lit a fire under me, or rather, between my legs. I was hell bent and determined to have sex--and not awkward sex either. Steamy, passionate sex. I marched into a little dive bar on one of the side streets in the French Quarter. Still close to Bourbon Street but not in the most trafficked section, this was a place where, by the stares and the inordinately loud greetings, you knew you were with the locals. I love New Orleans locals. They are a unique bunch, inextricably bound by tragedy. They are, above all else, New Orleanians. There are racial tensions and extreme wealth disparities, but the city as a whole comes together as one frequently in a near-constant state of celebration. Be it life, death, triumph, or tragedy, they celebrate. There is a unity among New Orleanians I have never seen among any other geographically connected group in the country.

I scouted the place for an eligible bachelor before making my way to the courtyard bar. For the first time in my life, I was turned on. Fired up. I finally understood what the word horny meant. I had been aroused before, but it was almost always in response to a guys' advances. I had never experienced such a primal desire for an orgasm until that night. I saw a few potential suitors, but no one really caught my attention until I sat at the bar. The bartender was a tall, thirty-something guy dressed in a casual button down top and dark jeans. His arms were lean and muscular. His attractiveness was seemingly effortless with his hazel eyes and messy sandy brown hair. He oozed sensuality. We made eye contact a few times while I waited and watched him work. Finally, he came over and asked if he could get me anything. I asked him for recommendations and he pointed out his favorites on the drink menu. The tension between us was palpable.

"Can I get a dirty martini?" I whisper-yelled into his ear, hoping he could hear me over the DJ.

"Vodka or gin?" He whisper-yelled back into mine, sending pulses of nervous energy through my body.

"Vodka" I said slowly. I didn't have a preference, but the word vodka kept my lips grazing his cheeks a millisecond longer. He felt my breath in his ear, and his eyes locked on mine, and I knew right then that I would know what he felt like inside me before the night was over.

Until I glanced at his hand and noticed a wedding ring. I wanted him, but I wasn't a home-wrecker, or as my grand-mother would say, a Bathsheba.

I stopped flirting with the bartender, but he kept showing interest in me. He became difficult to resist. He was one of the hottest people I had ever seen up close, and he wanted me. I could always tell when guys were into my friends, but never when they were into me. This guy though, I couldn't just see his desire, I could feel it, and it was making me wet.

The question "So, how married are you?" flowed from my mouth without my consent. I hoped he didn't hear me.

"Separated," he responded. "I'm still holding out hope, but she's already with someone else."

I almost replied, "Oh thank God," before realizing that's not a nice thing to say about someone's marriage falling apart. When he handed me my second martini, our fingers touched. I wanted him like I had never wanted anyone before.

Before I knew it I was up against a wall in the bar's back office, practically ripping off his shirt while his hands freely roamed my body. He hiked up my skirt and I hopped up on his desk, spreading my legs. I gripped the back of his hair as we began to fuck. Papers and trinkets were falling off the desk onto the floor. Nothing deterred us, not even when the DJ walked in, saw my heels in the air, and quickly backed out. For the first time in my life, I got lost in the throes of passion. I finally believed, at least in that moment, that sex was designed for pleasure; that sex was created to be enjoyed. And enjoy it, I did.

"I'm glad I didn't abort mission," I sighed to myself as I walked out of the bar, not looking back for a name or number. He was just "the bartender". No tears were shed in my bathtub that night, and I slept without regret.

Chapter Four

FRESH FACED

"HEY THERE." I WAS ALERTED TO SOCIAL MEDIA BY THE DING on my phone. Before I could decide whether or not to reply, a second message came through. It was Jacob. "I hope you don't mind me reaching out."

"Of course not!" I responded, following my message with a winky face emoji. I was getting into dangerous territory. But then again, I reasoned, he thinks I'm here simply on a writing assignment. He has no idea I'm here to explore my sexual desires, and he definitely doesn't know he's at the top of my list.

"What's your schedule like this weekend?"

"I don't know, why?" I was trying to play it cool, but the idea of Jacob being in my life after all this time, and under these circumstances had me shook. Was it meant to be? A gift from God? A temptation from the devil? I had come so far from my roots, but anytime I really wanted to do something, I still had to remind myself that wanting something didn't automatically mean it was bad for me.

"I'm shooting at Essence Fest, I'm allowed to bring one assistant."

"Well, good thing I've kept up with my photography skills!" I hoped that wasn't an awkward thing to say. We had taken photography lessons together when we were dating, bonding over our shared passion. I had always felt a sense of pride over him turning photography into a profession, as if I had a little something to do with it.

"Great! I can pick you up, or if it's easier for you, you can meet me at the convention center at 8:00am Friday."

"Could you pick me up?" I asked, reasoning with myself that I should ride with him to save money.

The week leading up to the gig was a blur of researching, signing up to work with Habitat for Humanity, and meeting with local historians. Even though it was a cover, the story on Post-Katrina New Orleans during hurricane season was a real job I had to do. It would be my consolation prize if this whole marriage vacation thing ended up destroying my life.

Despite my hectic week, I woke up early Friday morning bright eyed and fresh faced, eager to go spend the day with Jacob.

I was so excited I answered his phone call with "Hey, you here?"

"No," he said, "My booking got canceled due to a scheduling error. We're not going to be photographing anything today; we only have access to tomorrow's event." I could tell he was annoyed. "Any chance you're free tomorrow?" he asked.

Disappointed, I told him I couldn't because I had made arrangements to take a swamp tour.

"A swamp tour? You've got to be kidding me. I love it! You're going for the true local experience, huh?"

"It's part of my research, silly!"

"Okay. If for whatever reason your tour gets cancelled or something, let me know. I really could use the help."

I told him I'd see what I could do. I needed some time to think because I was still torn over whether it was a good idea to spend time together or not. Ultimately, I decided to go for it.

"Oh my, you are a sight for sore eyes!" Jacob said the next morning, hugging me for what seemed like a little longer than necessary. "I do most of my own work these days, but the financial security that the event company gives me is nice" Jacob said. "Unfortunately, it comes with mishaps like yesterday. Sorry about that. I'm so glad you could come today."

He gave me my instructions and equipment and then, to my surprise, sent me on my way. We didn't see each other much at all the rest of the day. Though I went expecting to work, I was bummed, as I'd hoped we'd at least hang out a little. I told myself it was for the best to not spend too much time with Jacob. The delicious food, amazing speakers, and great music at the event helped cheer me up.

"Here's your compensation for the evening, madam," Jacob said to me at the end of the night, handing me an envelope. My eyes grew wide when I opened it and saw the stack of money inside.

"And that's just your cut!" he joked. "Care to celebrate the end of a long and confusing couple of days?" Jacob asked. He must have sensed my inner turmoil.

"I'm meeting up with a few other workers for drinks," he said, in what seemed like an effort to let me know this invitation was platonic. I reminded myself why I was in New Orleans: to figure out sex and sexuality. That mission was too important to get side-tracked with unresolved feelings. But I couldn't say no, so I did a lot of mental gymnastics to convince myself it was okay to hang out with him.

The group, brought together simply by working the same event, was quite eclectic and extremely fun to be around. There was Aaron, the live painter from Milwaukee; Erin, also known as DJ Prada-G; and Nate, the bartender. We all had different stories and different backgrounds, but we got along famously.

I drank a little too much and laughed a little too hard. At one point I spilled my drink, which wasn't unusual having been voted "Most Likely to Trip On Stage at Graduation" my senior year of high school. When the night was over, Jacob drove me home, walked me to my door, and helped me remain standing as I fumbled in my purse for my keys. I may have been overly touchy with him as he tucked me in before returning to his car and driving away.

I closed my eyes and tried to sleep, but the room wouldn't stop spinning. Moments after Jacob left, I was curled over the toilet, remembering why I don't usually drink that much. As I sat with my head against the bathroom wall after emptying the contents of my stomach, vivid images of my youth played through my mind, as though I were watching a movie of my life.

SCENE: Summer morning, inside parents' house. 16-year-old Hillary enters the living room.

"What smells so good?" She asks through her yawn. Before anyone can answer, Hillary is rummaging through the brown paper bag, rustling the wrappers to find her favorite breakfast sandwich.

Not ten minutes after inhaling a sausage biscuit with cheese, Hillary becomes nauseous; a few minutes later, she vomits. Her parents, assuming it's a stomach bug, send her to bed, checking in every so often. As the day goes on she shivers under her covers from chills brought on from fever.

By early evening, it becomes clear that this is not a typical stomach bug. Her pain grows worse. Fearing dehydration, Hillary's dad drives her to the hospital. The rest of the night is a blur of green scrubs, bright lights, and vomiting bile into the hospital restroom. At some point in the night, a sense of urgency fills the air. A team of medical professionals move in and out of the triage room.

Too disoriented from the pain to fully grasp what's happening, she hears the words "ruptured appendix", and before she knows it, she is wheeled into the operating room and a mask is being lowered onto her face.

/END SCENE

The summer before senior year, my appendix burst, forcing me to undergo emergency surgery and preventing me from going on my church's youth trip. We'd been scheduled to leave the day after I got out of the hospital. A medical emergency which, in my mind, could only be seen as an act of God, prevented me from going on a church trip. The entire experience challenged many of my preconceived notions.

Did God not want me to go on this trip? Had I been sinning? Was my heart not "right with God"? Being given a medical emergency instead of a weekend of worshipping and fellowshipping seem to communicate loud and clear how little I mattered to God. I didn't realize it at the time, but this experience was the beginning of my deconstruction.

Chapter Five

GIRL FRIENDS

"DEAR THEO, I MISS YOU BEYOND WORDS."

One rainy afternoon, I sat on my front porch swing and wrote Theo a letter. I told him everything going on in my life. The awkward sex, the great sex, the stirrings I was having about Jacob. I told him how no one compared to him, but I wasn't sure if we were meant to be. I told him I was scared to lose him, but that I was more worried about losing myself. I wiped the tears off the letter and placed it in my dresser then pulled myself together, remembering I made plans for that evening with my friend Keira.

I met Keira on social media before I moved to NOLA. She was so helpful in answering questions I had about the city, and we bonded over our political ideologies and love of the outdoors. She was different from me in so many ways, but a kindred spirit. A single mom, born and raised in New Orleans, Keira was a few years older than me and had lived an extraordinary life. Even though I hadn't known her long, and hadn't even met her in person, she gained my trust almost immediately. Keira was unlike any other woman I had ever known.

When I was growing up, girls were the worst. I preferred the company of boys, not because I was boy crazy (and I definitely was). With boys, I always knew where I stood. I once got into a fist fight with a boy, and a few minutes after punching him square in the mouth we were friends again. In girl-world, if I ever stepped out of line with an off the cuff remark or something that came across as selfish, I was branded for life. I realized quickly that I couldn't make any mistakes, and I never really knew who my friends were. When a female classmate at my Christian school asked if I needed prayer about anything, it often meant she had heard a rumor about me and was using the guise of prayer to try to pry into my personal business.

Keira wasn't like that. She was a straight shooter who never gave a compliment she didn't mean. I think she clung to me because she wanted a friend who wasn't always talking about "hashtag momlife" as she called it. She had lost herself in motherhood and was dying to figure out who she was now as a single and successful modern woman and mother. Despite struggling to find her new footing, she was rocking at life. Keira remained more focused on the present, whereas my mind bounced back and forth between the past and the future. I didn't know it then, but Keira was instrumental in my learning to see the beauty in the moment.

"You could use a little meat on your bones." Keira said, wiggling my bony hips. She was right. In those days I really did have trouble putting on weight, and I was thinner than I wanted to be. I was thankful for the curious way New Orleanians could deep fry just about anything, making even healthy foods bad for you, yet oh so delicious. Plus, no one hosted a get-together of any kind without alcohol, be it through the open bar or the inclusion of "BYOB" on the invitation.

"I'm trying", I told Keira, gently pushing her hand away and shoving a jalapeño popper in my mouth--deep fried, of course.

I wanted to tell her what I was really doing there, about all the marital issues Theo and I had, all the months we spent in counseling trying to make it work. I wanted to let her in on my struggle to understand sex and sexuality and tell her about our unorthodox plan to save our marriage. I wanted to tell her so much, but I had to vet her carefully before divulging any sensitive information. After all, I had learned that girls weren't trustworthy.

Growing up being burned by girls I thought were my friends, I was jaded. I couldn't believe a person as genuine as Keira existed. Maybe once women became mothers they stopped being so catty, judgmental, and competitive? Or maybe Keira was a unicorn. She seemed to have a more masculine temperament inside her female, womanly exterior. She spoke her mind. She didn't care about impressing anyone, wasn't bothered by people's opinions, and remained humble despite her accomplishments.

"People are just people, but all people are people", she'd say. She treated everyone with respect and dignity, but didn't favor any one type of person over another.

Keira and I could talk about deep issues such as wealth inequality, intersectional feminism, and the afterlife, then easily transition to discussing our love of tacos, over the knee boots, and reality TV. Only this night, I could barely keep focused on anything except Theo. Sensing I was lost in my thoughts, Keira asked me if I wanted to call it a night right after we finished our first round of drinks.

"I'm fine. I'm just really missing home right now." I told her.

"Well, it's up to you. I have a sitter until 9:00 so I wanna stay out, but you don't have to entertain me. I'll find something or someone to keep me busy."

"Do you want to just come over?" I asked, realizing Keira had never been to my house.

"Sure!"

"Man, I need to get a car," I told her as she navigated through the one-ways, trying to avoid ever present road construction that lined the streets along the route from downtown to my shotgun double.

"What a great place!" she exclaimed, setting down her purse and raiding my fridge like she lived there. I loved how comfortable she was with me, with herself, with life in general.

Keira and I slipped off our shoes, wrapped throw blankets over our shoulders and curled up on my sofa for some trashy reality TV. Before long, we began stuffing our faces with the mint chocolate chip ice cream I had bought earlier that week because it reminded me of Theo. He's not a big ice cream fan, but mint chocolate chip is his favorite. A little comfort eating would be just what I needed, and having Keira share it with me was a bonus. I was so tempted to open up to her and tell her why I was really in New Orleans. I told her a little about my evangelical upbringing, which is hard to do to an outsider. She never made me feel judged, but what would she think if she knew I had a date with a guy I met on a dating app later that night? Would she judge me? When I eventually told her the truth, I wasn't at all prepared for her reaction.

Chapter Six

FIRST DATE

"YOU OKAY?" HE ASKED, HIS VOICE TELLING ME HE DIDN'T HAVE to see my trembling hands to know I was a ball of nerves. I just couldn't believe my attractive, intelligent, and effortlessly hilarious friend would be romantically interested in me.

"I'm sorry. The truth is I'm a nervous wreck." I confessed.

Oh my god why did I blurt that out?!

"It's okay. I'm nervous, too." He tried to reassure me, but his confidence told me he wasn't nearly as nervous as I.

My cheeks turned bright red. He made me feel vulnerable, almost against my will. Everything he said was coated with a humble acceptance I had never experienced.

"Hillary, I am fascinated with you. I've never met anyone quite like you. Since we first met, my feelings for you have continued to grow, and being on this date with you means a lot to me, but I expect some level of awkwardness as we begin taking our friendship to the next level."

I couldn't make eye contact, but I could feel his big brown eyes trying to connect with mine.

"You're right." I replied, shifting around in my seat, wondering how Theo was so comfortable with the topic at hand. "What are you thinking of ordering?" I gazed over the menu, trying to shift the conversation away from my sweaty palms.

I was replaying my first date with Theo in my mind, realizing it was nothing like the first date I was currently on that muggy, New Orleans evening. Sure, my current date and I were also not making eye contact, but this time my nerves were replaced with annoyance because this douche-canoe wouldn't stop talking himself.

I didn't care that he graduated from some elite school. And I certainly didn't care how much his parents were worth. To my surprise, I was laser focused on his body, wondering if the cross country scholarship he wouldn't stop talking about kept him in good shape.

Who had I become? I didn't care about Bennett or his Tesla. My feelings toward him were, at best, a blend of disdain and pity, yet I kept picturing him in my bedroom. The girl I was when I left Austin would have never behaved this way. Though I still had some insecurities, I was getting used to my newfound self-assuredness and sexual liberation.

"Do you want to come in for a drink?" I asked, knowing that Bennett lived such a phony life he wouldn't be able to handle the truth. I fantasized about telling him the truth, though.

"You're an alright guy, but you're so insecure and all these things you accumulate only impress women just as empty and vapid as you are. After I have my way with you, I will never want to see you again."

He was trying to act so smooth. Name dropping, showing off his pricey watch, ordering the most expensive bottle of wine at the restaurant. I let him flaunt his money so he could remain under the illusion he was great at getting girls into bed. I knew his M.O. Though my experience was limited, I had been propositioned by guys like Bennett in the past. This was my first time being open to sex with a guy I not only wasn't married to, but didn't particularly like. I chuckled a little at the realization Bennett would think he closed the deal with his stellar performance then never call me again.

After giving him a quick tour of my house, I excused myself to put on something more comfortable which really just meant an outfit that showed more skin. I emerged braless in my Keep Austin Weird tank and my black cotton skirt. I poured us each a glass of wine and sat next to him on the couch.

"I like your outfit," he told me, running one finger along the strap of my tank top.

"Oh, this old thing?" I said. In a less than smooth move, I went on to explain how the shirt really was old and I bought it at a street fair in Austin way back before I even moved there.

The touch of his hand sent a chill through my body. "Well, it looks really good on you," he said. It took all of my willpower not to straddle him right there on the couch.

"Did I tell you I'm taking massage therapy classes?" Bennett, who suddenly became way more interesting, asked me.

"You did not," I replied, leaning in closer to him, giving him my best "tell me more" eyes.

"Yeah, I wanted to study kinesiology in college, but my family business required me to be a business major and get my MBA. Massage is the closest I can get at this point in my life." That was probably the most genuine thing he said to me.

"Well, if you ever need a body to practice on, I volunteer as a tribute." I said, hoping that wasn't too forward. He agreed and offered to give me a massage right then and there.

I turned away from him and scooted my back closer to his body. I took all my hair and moved it over to the side, exposing my back and my little flower tattoo.

"That's cute," he said, slowly running his finger across my tattoo and down my back.

"Thanks," I replied, turning my face to his. We were mere inches apart. After a lustful glance, I turned back and adjusted my shoulders so he could begin the massage. He pushed his fingers and thumbs into my back and shoulders, and I began to get lost in pleasure.

"How's the pressure?" He whispered.

"It's grrrrrreat." I arched my back and moaned.

His hands began to wander a little. First down to the small of my back. Then to my hips and he reached around to caress my inner thigh before tugging on the bottom of my tank top and whispering in my ear, "I could do such a better job if you let me take this off."

"Is that how you're taught to massage people? Topless?" I questioned.

"Only for clients who get the full treatment." He teased, lifting my tank top over my head.

"Well, if you're offering, I want the full treatment." I said, leaning my half naked body into his chest.

I think we had such great sexual chemistry because I didn't like him very much, so I was less reserved, and that made for really good sex. Every kiss, every caress between the two of us was smooth and effortless. His skills in the bedroom (well, technically on my sofa) were brag-worthy.

The next morning, I woke up to the clanking sound of him buckling his belt. As soon as our eyes met, he began fumbling with his pants zipper and tripping over an apology. He said he needed to run, that he had a "really busy day" ahead of him. He kissed my cheek, told me he'd call me and quickly walked out the door.

Narrator: "And she never heard from Bennett again."

My first date with Theo didn't end with sex. It didn't even end with a kiss, only a hug. All it took was that one date for me to realize I was head over heels in love with Theo. Theo was, in a way, the anti-Bennett. There was zero pretense about him. He could afford nice things, but chose to live simply. He didn't seek recognition for all his good works, and he certainly didn't get caught up in the rat race. Of everyone I had ever known, Theo gave the least amount of fucks about what anyone thought of him.

Our relationship was built of the kind of trust and camaraderie that comes from true friendship. Even though I had moved away from Evangelicalism when we met, I still held onto the beliefs purity culture instilled in me. Little did I know, that decision would cause me more heartache and inner turmoil than I could handle. Ironically, engaging in meaningless, casual sex was healing me of my deep-seeded shame.

Chapter Seven

HOME SICK

"SEE YOU TONIGHT!" KEIRA TEXTED ME.

"Yay!!! Can't wait!" I had a bad habit of over-compensating for my lack of enthusiasm with exclamation points. I reluctantly got dressed, putting on a flowy black skirt, a white t-shirt with 504, the New Orleans area code, printed in gold across the chest, and my gold flip flops.

It was the 4th of July, and I was missing Theo more than ever. This was the first time in years that we wouldn't be watching fireworks together in Downtown Austin. Instead, I was meeting Keira, her daughter, and some of her friends to watch fireworks, or "fy-ah-wok" as Keira's daughter called them, along the Mississippi River.

Meeting Keira's daughter was bittersweet. I loved kids. I really thought I would have one by the time I was 30, yet I stood there on that hot night at almost 28 years old, facing possible divorce with no prospects of children in my life.

"You have time," Keira said, as if she could read my thoughts. "I was 31 when Quinn was born."

Keira was trying to be helpful, and I appreciated it. But she had no idea about the real reason I didn't have kids. She didn't know I was in New Orleans trying to discover my "inner sexual goddess" as Betsy, my therapist back in Austin, had suggested. Well, she didn't explicitly say I needed to sleep with a bunch of people, but she said I needed to own my sexuality and get over my body shaming and slut shaming mentality. Unfortunately, I wasn't able to do that in my bedroom with my husband.

Just as the fireworks began to pop, tears fell from my eyes. I pulled myself together long enough to tell Keira I was leaving.

"I'm sorry. I'm just really homesick tonight." Being vulnerable like that was hard, but Keira knew exactly how to handle my feelings. She hugged me warmly and encouraged me to go home and get some rest.

As I walked away, I couldn't help but feel disappointed about being too sad to enjoy a night out with other women. Her friends were hilarious and down to earth, but I couldn't get out of my head enough to have fun.

I didn't really want to go home. I wanted to be distracted with drinks and camaraderie and a fireworks display, but I felt like a wet blanket. I thought after more than a month in New Orleans I would have a better understanding of sex and my relationship with it. I had learned to enjoy sex, and I was a little more comfortable with my naked body, but I still wrestled with guilt. I wasn't sure if I should stop until I no longer felt like a horrible slut. In my mind, an act of immense pleasure between two consenting adults somehow still caused the woman to be tattered and ruined in the eyes of the Lord. I didn't actually agree with these misogynistic beliefs, but I couldn't shake the shame around my sex life.

I did volunteer work. I spoke out about injustices. I wrote articles that changed hearts and minds. I treated people with compassion. I loved big. I saw myself as a good person who loved my neighbor as myself, and unlike the religious people in the parable of the Good Samaritan, I don't ask who my neighbor is. I know that every fellow human is my neighbor. Why did they teach us that was sex was bigger than everything else?

"Whyyyyyyyyy?" I fell face first into my pillow and cried out as loud as I could. "Why am I so messed up?" I wondered. My sadness soon turned to anger. Was God even there? Why did the church tell me God cared so much about my sex life? I don't recall Jesus saying nearly as much about sex as he did about social justice. I was pissed off that night. In the moment, I felt compelled to have sex in reaction to the frustration I was experiencing. I paid close attention to those feelings because I was there to heal myself, not become a sex addict.

As if on cue, I got an unexpected text from Jacob.

"Can you meet me for a drink?"

He had no idea how hard it would be for me to contain myself around him. But I knew he wouldn't text me unless it was about something serious.

"Sure."

Twenty minutes later, we were at an Uptown dive bar near Tulane University, munching on French fries and bullshitting about our weeks.

"Is everything okay?" I asked, taking a more serious tone.

He took a swig of beer before replying, "Yeah, I just needed to get out of my head tonight."

"Wanna go somewhere and talk?" I asked him. The bar was more crowded than normal because of the 4th of July holiday.

We walked around Tulane's campus a little while before Jacob broke down and told me his ex-wife, Janelle, was getting remarried.

"I know it's been a year, but it's only been a year, ya know, Hil," Jacob lamented. He had hardly mentioned Janelle since we reconnected. I knew they were divorced, but didn't know the details and hadn't asked any questions. I figured he would talk to me about it if he wanted to. Knowing I wasn't divulging much about my relationship, I didn't think it wise to probe him for information.

"I know. I'm so sorry." I tried to offer encouragement, reminding him how normal it was to have lingering feelings, encouraging him on how far he'd come.

"You chased your dreams and became a successful photographer; you live in the best city. You have a lot to celebrate!" I told him with as much enthusiasm as I could muster.

"I don't even miss her. I didn't see how unhappy we were in our marriage. I'm thankful she left, because I never would have. But I can't believe this is my reality."

"I understand. It's hard to see what's wrong in our lives when so much of our lives are wrong," I said, trying to be helpful. I'm not even sure what I meant.

"I just...this isn't where I thought I would be. I never wanted to be divorced. I did everything right."

"Believe me, I know how you feel," I told him.

"Yeah, right. You and Theo have a great relationship... Don't you?" He asked, unsure of the status of my relationship.

"We are far from perfect," I confessed. "We are actually working through some of our own issues while I'm here."

"Oh, Hillary, I'm sorry." Jacob rested his hand on my shoulder and a surge of longing raced down my spine. "What kind of issues?" he asked. I could tell he didn't want to be alone in his pain. I wanted to tell him everything, but I was too afraid.

"Just typical husband/wife issues," I said, unwilling to open up further.

The clear, full moon and unusual lack of humidity lent to the tenderness of the moment between us. In our shared pain, we sought comfort in one another. We stared into each other's eyes and I thought this would be it. I thought we would start to kiss before we lowered ourselves to the ground where I would sit on his lap, facing him. I thought he would lift up my skirt to discover I wasn't wearing any panties. I thought this would be the night I learned what Jacob felt like inside me.

I don't know what would have happened that night if we were given the chance. Instead, a security officer shined her light in our faces, asking us to show our ID's or leave the campus.

I didn't get anywhere with Jacob that night. Instead, I walked into my shotgun double alone, just before the sun came up the morning of July 5th.

Chapter Eight

LOVING MYSELF

I'M GETTING RESTLESS. I NEED TO SNAP MYSELF OUT OF THIS debilitating frustration. I penned those words in my journal in early July.

I realized I hadn't spent any time in nature since arriving in New Orleans, so I booked a cabin for the weekend at a local state park. I needed some time away from my new normal to really figure out what I was doing there, plus I could start organizing some of the information I gathered for my Katrina piece.

I had been in New Orleans for over a month. So far I'd slept with three people. I had one awkward and two good experiences, one of them so good I still get tingly when I think about it. Yet none of them yielded meaningful change in who I was. *Unless you count me no longer giving a shit about sex something worth noting,* I thought to myself, not realizing how much progress I had made just by thinking such a thing.

The State Park was serene. The marshlands, the lake, the

birds flying overhead.   Aside from a couple of families strolling by here and there, I was alone on the trail's lookout point.

"Look out. Breathe in. Take a moment just to exist." –Robert California

Those words, penned into the unfinished wood railing I leaned on, unnerved me. I didn't know how to be in the moment and just exist. In my attempt to save my marriage and figure out sex, plus my efforts to compartmentalize my life, looking to the past and wondering about the future had me more thrown off than I was back in Austin. I had to make some changes. In that moment, I relished my existence and the solitude around me.

The cabins were few and far between, so I was basically on my own. I decided to eat a weed gummy bear Keira had given me a couple weeks earlier. "You'll love it; I promise" she'd assured me. I was nervous because I hadn't smoked pot since high school, and I had never taken an edible. Looking back, I realize how ill-advised it was to do a drug I hadn't done in more than 10 years while I was alone in the woods.

The high was mild, but it freed my mind. I put on a guided meditation track I had thumbed through earlier, thinking I wouldn't be able to follow anything given my state of mind.

My body relaxed into the bed. The music started and my senses awakened. I felt overcome with desire. I knew I was capable of taking care of myself, but I had never done that before. Beyond having any and all sexual thoughts shamed out of me before I could have them, I had an unnatural worry that my great-grandparents were watching me from heaven. I'm aware of how ridiculous it is now, but growing up believing that masturbation was worse than sex, and sex was pretty much the worst sin you could commit, really impacted my ability to see sexual desire as normal.

In the cabin, though, I was too high to think about my dead relatives judging me from the afterlife, so I allowed my curiosity to take over.

I licked my lips and slowly ran my fingers across my chest, then down my stomach to my inner thigh, allowing my fingertips to graze my panties. Thoughts were momentarily suspended while my feelings took center stage. My hands acted like they were operating independent of my mind. They knew just what to do. I spent what felt like an eternity exploring my body, bringing myself mere inches from orgasm then backing off. I knew myself better than I thought. I knew what I liked. I knew what I wanted. I didn't need Theo, Jacob, Bennett or any guy for that matter. At that moment, I was only concerned with myself. As I was finishing, I let out an involuntary moan of pleasure and when I opened my eyes, the world around me was more vivid, as if until that moment I had been living my life in black and white. All I needed was one good orgasm to bring me into technicolor. While I lay there, spent and satisfied, I heard rustling outside. Maybe it was a neighbor. It could have been a grizzly bear for all I knew; I was in a euphoria of my own making, and nothing could break me of it.

Well, nothing except the annoyingly high pitched yet endearing sound of children playing. The sun was coming up and the neighboring family had just begun their day, which included parents yelling at their kids to stop being so loud.

I was still in awe of how intense my orgasm was the night before. I had never felt so free. I found myself wishing I had felt that free with Theo. Or anyone, really. Until that night in the cabin I didn't know I could be that free at all. Before, on the rare occasions I would masturbate, it was rushed, like an urge I could no longer contain, and I had to get to the release as quickly as possible. I woke up that day a new woman. One who knew how to make herself feel good.

Hiking was different than the day before. Nearly all the other campers drove off that morning, and I hiked virtually alone on the trail. Reverence filled the air during my walk. I stood in awe of nature, and how she needs nothing from us to exist.

Upon leaving the cabin, I vowed to focus on myself. To love, please, and care for me. Everything I had been doing had been for Theo as much as it had been for me. I was trying to cure my sexual shame and traumas to save my marriage, but it was time to work on myself for my own sake. I started therapy and spent the next several weeks focusing on writing and working with Habitat for Humanity, only seeing Jacob or Keira occasionally.

Chapter Nine

TALK THERAPY

"I THOUGHT THINGS WOULD GET BETTER, BUT MY PROBLEMS only got worse. I thought marriage was the antidote to the anxiety and shame I carried around sex and sexuality. I waited until I was married to officially have sex, but I was still ashamed of my body. The only difference was that once I got married, someone else was subject to my trauma. Theo tried, but he couldn't understand. He didn't care what I had or hadn't done. He had his own colorful sexual past and was unbothered by it. The fact that he had multiple sexual partners before he met me didn't concern him. I, on the other hand, hated knowing he had been with other women. I wasn't jealous of them as much as jealous of Theo for being sexually liberated. For crying out loud, he told his mom when he lost his virginity at the ripe old age of fifteen! To this day I don't talk to my parents about sex. Growing up, the sex talk in my house was limited to biology and purity on the rare occasion anything sexual was discussed. My parents told me the mechanics and that people have sex to make babies. I got the message loud and clear: sex was to please my husband, though no one came out and said those words to me. We were told we had to wait until marriage to be counted as pure in the eyes of not just God, but our dads and our future husbands too. Then, as we got to our late teens, the conversation shifted to how women should approach sex as wives. We were all but directly told to give our husbands what they wanted, when they wanted it. Our desires or pleasure never came up."

"And how did that make you feel?" Jill, my New Orleans therapist asked me in her deliberately non-judgmental voice. Jill was around my age, married with a step-daughter. She was smart, funny, and an all-around badass. I still wish we had met under different circumstances so we could be friends. Then again, that would mean she wouldn't have been my therapist, and I needed a good therapist.

"It made me feel subhuman." I told her. "It made me feel like my worth was only in how valuable I was to someone else. What about *me*? Wasn't I valuable to the world just because I existed? Why is there so much talk about sexual sin and so little talk about other things that impact us? Why didn't they talk to us about protecting the environment or offer any volunteer opportunities that didn't require us to ask the communities we helped to accept Christianity? Why couldn't we just help people where they were and show them love, without conditions?"

"You seem angry. What is making you angry?" Jill probed, forcing me to look deeper.

"I'm angry because they fucking robbed me of my life!!!" I sobbed.

"What do you mean?" she asked, not being satisfied with general answers.

My fists were trembling with fury by this point.

"They told me I was only as good as they deemed me. I was only valuable if a man saw me as valuable. My dreams, my wants, my desires paled in comparison to my future husband's, if they mattered at all. The church pretty much told me the less sexual I was, the closer to God I could be. But I wasn't close to God at all! I tried. Everything. I did everything right. But I still suffered intense shame and guilt each time Theo and I had sex, as if I were impure. Sure, I gave Jacob a hand job once, but that wasn't sex. It shouldn't have made me feel so much guilt that I broke up with him, right?"

"Wait, who's Jacob?" She asked. I'm not sure if she needed to know, or if she was buying time to figure out how to deal with everything I'd blurted out mere minutes after meeting her.

"He was my high school boyfriend, a fellow youth leader in the church. We were getting way too physical, causing each other to stumble, so I broke up with him the summer before freshman year of college," I told her, using air quotes when I said, "causing each other to stumble."

"Did you guys love each other?" She asked.

"I guess, as much as you could love someone at seventeen," I told her. I hadn't thought about my love for Jacob back then. It was immature, but it was genuine.

"Can you tell me a little about this relationship that you were compelled to end?"

I let out a deep sigh as the memories of our time together came rushing back.

"We met in eighth grade. I liked him then, and I learned later that he liked me too, but like the popular purity book suggested, we had "kissed dating goodbye", so we were just friends for a while. By the time 10th grade rolled around, most of our youth group had found a way around the "no dating" rule we all placed on ourselves, and everyone started "courting".

"Kissed dating goodbye? Courting?" She interrupted, unable to hide her utter confusion. I may as well have been speaking Greek.

"Our youth group was taught to kiss dating goodbye in a book that was all the rage when I was coming up. Courting was essentially the same thing as dating, but guys were only supposed to court girls they thought they might want to marry. Of course, courting was really just a workaround the no-dating culture."

Jill sat with a blank stare for a moment, trying to process the fact that I grew up in an alternate reality, and now I was on this Earth trying to figure out how to engage in healthy human relationships.

"So, was anything wrong in this, courtship, as you call it, when you broke up with Jacob?"

"Yes, we were getting too close to having sex," I reminded her.

"Was he pressuring you to have sex?" Concern growing in her voice.

"No way. He was always respectful."

"Did he treat you poorly?" I could see her wheels spinning

as she tried to figure out the problem that led me to break up with Jacob.

"No, not at all."

"And so, you broke up because you were enjoying each other too much that you thought you might have sex?" It was becoming increasingly difficult for Jill to hide her true feelings.

"Yes." I said, fully realizing just how ridiculous it sounded. I broke up with a great guy because we were too physical with each other.

"Listen, I hear you and I know this is your truth and your reality, but what they taught you was fucked up."

"I KNOW! Thank you for saying that. It's.... validating," I said, sitting across from her on a cozy black couch, my face showing a mixture of pride and embarrassment. Proud, because deep down I always knew it was messed up. My worth was far more than what my church leaders reduced me to. I was not simply a vagina to be preserved for a husband. I was smart, strong, funny, and capable. I didn't need approval from the church leaders, but for so long I thought I did.

"I'm sorry," Jill continued. "I normally wouldn't be so blunt on the first visit, but I feel your pain and am frustrated for you. You deserve to see yourself as worthy."

I knew right then that I would get my money's worth out of talk therapy.

Chapter Ten

VOLUNTARY EVACUATION

"You all packed?" The text came through on an early August morning just as I was digging out my suitcase.

"Yeah." I lied.

"Be there in 20." As soon as I saw that text, I started running around like a chicken with my head cut off trying to pack for a weekend away.

A few weeks earlier, Keira and I had made plans for a quick trip to the gulf coast. We were only 3.5 hours away from the white, sandy beaches of the Emerald Coast so we figured, why not enjoy a mini-vacation?

Narrator: "Because it's hurricane season, that's why not."

The week of our trip we learned a Tropical Storm was threatening the Florida Coast. We made what ended up being a stupid decision to cancel our room, not wanting to risk losing the $200 deposit we put down.

I spent a lot of time that week thinking about Jacob. We were together during Hurricane Katrina, offering resources and supplies to displaced families. We had a pretty sizable influx of evacuees we opened our hearts and homes to, even though Austin didn't get the kind of national media coverage that Houston and Dallas did.

I kept replaying the recent conversation with my therapist. Was she trying to tell me something? Jacob and I broke up so I could stay pure, but the whole culture of purity was wrong and based on outdated, patriarchal systems. If we had grown up differently, would we have broken up then? Or ever? Would Theo and I have even met?

These were my ponderings when the news alert popped up on my phone. The tropical storm had strengthened into a Category 1 hurricane and changed course. All signs now pointed to New Orleans, and the city was under a voluntary evacuation.

All I really knew of hurricanes was Katrina, so I didn't know that a voluntary evacuation meant most people would stock up on bread and beer, fill their cars with gasoline and ride out the storm at home. I was trying to get someone to get me out of there. I scolded myself over my delay in getting a car, vowing to go car shopping as soon as I could.

"Are you staying or going?" I texted Keira, hoping I could either evacuate with her, or at the very least stay with her. I couldn't be alone for a hurricane. I was too afraid. Afraid of the levees. Afraid the federal government would, once again, forget about the city. I hadn't even experienced Katrina and I was a wreck. I wondered how the locals felt, and made a note to add this experience to my list of questions for people I interviewed.

"I have to go with Brad's family." She replied. She had a

good relationship with her ex, but man, evacuating with your ex-husband and former in-laws seems insane. Of course, I am the last person to judge someone. Maybe it was a good thing they could evacuate together and not kill each other. Or maybe she would hate every minute of her weekend. I didn't know what it meant for Keira, but it at least meant I wasn't going to be tagging along.

Before I knew it, Thursday had arrived and it was my last chance to get out of town before the hurricane made landfall. I considered catching a flight home, even though Theo and I weren't supposed to have any contact. These were extenuating circumstances.

I was surprised to hear from Jacob, considering I had distanced myself from him the last few weeks. I figured he would've made plans with his buddies, or that cute red headed woman he posted a photo of earlier that week.

"What are you doing for this storm?" he asked me.

"I guess I'm just staying home, hoping my roof doesn't blow off."

"It's only a category 1, you don't have to worry about your roof blowing away." He said it with such confidence, I began to feel a little better. After all, Jacob had lived there through one hurricane season already; he had to know more than I did about the risk.

"Your biggest concern will be flooding and power outages." There went my reassurance.

"If you want to avoid it all, I'm heading up to my cabin in Franklinton, you're welcome to join me."

I tried to hide my enthusiasm, but my emphatic, "YES, PLEASE!" probably gave me away.

We holed up in his cabin a couple hours north of the city, drinking, talking, and playing video games on his old school Super Nintendo. Jacob and I also talked a lot about our lives and marriages. I didn't open up too much about mine, but Jacob told me about his problems with Janelle and why they eventually split up. He told me about what had first brought him to New Orleans. He visited once, just before he got married, to attend his college roommate's wedding.

"And the city just captivated me. I soaked up as much culture as I could in the three days I was here, and when I left, a part of me stayed behind."

He went on to tell me that once his marriage fell apart, he knew he had to get out of Dallas where he had been living, and he didn't want to go back home to our small town outside of Austin.

"So, I packed my car, set my GPS to New Orleans and never looked back."

I was inspired by Jacob's ability to take charge of his life, even when things looked bleak.

Our last night in Franklinton, the conversation took us back to our time as a couple., something we hadn't discussed since we broke up. We bonded over our old favorite songs, laughed about our questionable wardrobe choices, and reminisced about how smitten we had been with each other.

"You were my first love," He whispered.

"You were mine," I admitted.

"I don't quite know what went wrong," Jacob confessed. "I figured I had done something."

"Well, kinda. I mean, it was more something I did... to you," I said, glaring at the zipper area of his pants.

"Oh, wait...*that*?"

"Yes, *that*." I shot back.

The look on his face told me that he had no idea why I would feel that us going that far would lead me to break up with him.

"I...I was really worried about us going too far and me not being pure anymore." I confessed.

"Oh my gosh... You took that stuff seriously?" He asked, completely surprised.

Of course I did. Didn't he know me at all?

"Very seriously." I retorted.

"All that true love waits stuff was just bullshit. Everyone in youth group was having sex. Or at least, they were telling everyone they were. I may have even lied about having sex with you in order to fit in..." His words trailed off.

Seething with rage, I yelled in a voice I didn't know I had, "You did WHAT??"

Jacob explained the pressure he faced as a teenager to be good at everything, including sports, school and of course he had to be a good Christian while trying to fit in with his peers who were either embellishing or outright lying about their experiences. He apologized profusely for lying about us.

We shed many tears as we opened old wounds and began healing from our past. I couldn't tell at the time if it was for better or worse, but something in our relationship shifted that weekend. I felt closer to Jacob, yet more awkward around him. We worked through issues I didn't know we had, and I came to realize just how connected we had become over the years. I was scared of what this might mean, so I pulled back. After we returned from Franklinton, I didn't talk to Jacob for almost three months.

Chapter Eleven

CAR SHOPPING

"CALL HIM NOW!" ANGELIQUE DEMANDED. "HE WANTS TO GET rid of it today."

I couldn't put it off any longer. I needed a car. New Orleans simply wasn't equipped for pedestrians, and their public transportation system left a lot to be desired. Tired of having to book a ride every time I wanted to leave the house, I had set off on a mission to find an affordable used car.

I had tried some car lots to no avail, and was ready to give up when I heard from my friend Angelique. She told me her sister was dating a lawyer who somehow ended up with a car he needed to get rid of. The owner had moved to Canada, and now this lawyer who was supposed to facilitate a sale was charged with selling it.

After making arrangements to meet the lawyer at his house, I found myself wondering if this was some sort of divine intervention. In my former life I would have immediately attributed this car falling into my lap as God's favor. But would that same God offer me, a married woman who was engaging in all sorts of extramarital sex, such a sweet deal on a 2004 Honda Civic?

"And yeah, it's a good little car, I just have no use for it," the lawyer, Sean, told me.

At a glance, it was clear that Sean was athletic. He was tall and lean, but muscular. His face even looked strong, like he was chiseled out of stone or something. He was a few years older than me, maybe in his late 30's. He broke all my stereotypes about lawyers. He had zero pretension, was hilarious, and didn't look like he had a lot of money.

"So, what kind of law do you practice?" I asked, making small talk that would hopefully cause me to sound like I knew a little more about the legal field than I actually did.

"I'm a public defender," he told me, which probably explained why he wasn't wealthy, but what did I know. I secretly hoped he was a public defender because he cared about criminal justice reform.

"I'm sorry, my notary buddy is running late. Do you want a cup of coffee--or," he looked at his watch, "it's after 5:00, how about a beer?"

I accepted his offer and we sat at his kitchen table. As we chatted, I learned that Sean was divorced with no children and had graduated from Louisiana State University where he went on a basketball scholarship, and he did, in fact, want to help improve the criminal justice system. As if that wasn't enough, his wit was sharp and charming. Whew.

Without warning, I started thinking about the two of us having sex. While he was telling me the story of how he got the car, I pictured him picking me up with his strong arms and pulling my body into his.

"It was a really friendly couple who taught at a local immersion school, so I didn't mind handling the paperwork for them..." I don't recall the details of his story.

As he spoke, I imagined my legs wrapped around his waist and him carrying me to his bedroom.

"And then, the sale fell through so I was stuck with this car that I have no use for."

I don't remember exactly what he was saying because I was too busy fantasizing about him taking off my underwear with his teeth.

"May I use your bathroom?" I interrupted his story to compose myself by splashing a little water on my face. I thought about taking care of myself in the restroom, but I was too nervous that he'd know what I was doing, or worse, think I was going number two.

"So, you were talking about how you got the car and the last sale falling through... How long have you had it now?" I probed, trying to get my head back in the conversation, but to this day I have no idea why the sale had fallen through.

"A few weeks. I had to get some paperwork cleared up before I could legally sell it, and I'll be able to once my notary friend gets here. I texted him again. I'm not sure what is taking him so long."

I was surprised at my level of comfort in this situation. Ordinarily, alarm bells would be sounding at the fact that I was alone at a strange guy's house after dark. But Sean wasn't strange, and he wasn't a total stranger. Still though, I declined when he offered me a second beer.

"Do you work with your notary friend?" I asked, in an effort to keep my mind off the fact that I would need to change my underwear as soon as I got home. It was hard not to think about having sex with him. I wondered if he was thinking about it too, though, I quickly shot down that wondering.

"Oh, no, we went to grad school together at..." Something, somewhere. I can't remember. I was watching the next soft-core porn movie Sean and I were starring in inside my head. I imagined standing from my chair, pushing it back so hard it clanked onto the floor as I walked over to Sean, turning his body toward mine and throwing one leg over each side of the chair, lowering myself onto his lap. I fantasized about grabbing his face and kissing him.

It was probably a good thing when his Notary friend, Jose, knocked on the door when he did. His presence got me out of my head and brought me back to the conversation.

The feeling of desire was still new and shocking to me. I wanted Sean. I didn't let him know, but I couldn't seem to stop the yearning I had for him. For the first time, I allowed myself to get carried away in a fantasy, and I had to admit, I liked it.

After a lively conversation with Sean and Jose that caused them to give me the nickname Moxie, I was driving back to my shotgun double in my new, insanely affordable car. The nickname Moxie made me feel strong. "Maybe I am a girl who has moxie," I thought to myself as I drove home, blaring Ani Difranco.

Chapter Twelve

CAGED BIRD

"HEY GIRL WHATCHA UP TO? I HEAR YOU'RE IN NOLA."

That's strange, I haven't heard from her in ages, I thought to myself when the text from Megan popped up. Megan Salinger was, without a doubt, the most spiritual Christian in the youth group. They say we are all equals in the eyes of the Lord, but we definitely ranked each other. Megan was the most spiritual, Tasha was the least, and the rest of us were somewhere in between. Like every other area of my life, I was painfully average, being more spiritual than the girls who smoked and certainly more than those who had sex, but less spiritual than the ones who hosted Bible studies and answered every "How are you?" with "Blessed."

When I read the words, "I hear you're in NOLA," my heart stopped. My mind raced with questions. "How does she know I'm here? Did she talk to Theo? Or Jacob, or worse? Could she have talked to Janelle, Jacob's ex-wife? I'm sure he told her he had seen me. What does she want from me?" My anxiety was quickly getting the best of me.

Her next message answered everything.

"I ran into Theo and he told me that u were there on assignment. I'm heading there for a conference & I'd love to try to meet up sometime this weekend for coffee if you have time!" Followed by a smiley face emoji.

For being in digital marketing, Megan sure knew how to speak casually via message.

"Sure. Sounds great!" I replied.

I did like Megan, but she was so... perfect. I know I shouldn't be upset about someone's lack of faults, but I mean, aside from her questionable sentence structure, she had no real flaws. She was pretty, kind, smart and loved Jesus so much. She seemed to have it all together, which annoyed me because there I was riding the struggle bus, flailing about, trying to reclaim some sense of sexual expression, and she was leaving her perfect Texas home she shared with her husband, Nathan, and her three adorable kids to spend a weekend at a tech conference, paid for, I assumed, by Google, where she worked. Our coffee date was as expected. We gave superficial updates on our lives and made small talk about work, family, and friends. She filled me in on what was happening at the Christian school attached to my old church.

"So once the new principal showed up with long hair, they had to rewrite the rules and the boys can now have long hair. Can you believe that?" She asked me in her thick southern drawl. I had known Megan since 8th grade and no matter how long she lived away from South Mississippi, she never lost her accent. I may have a bit of a Texas twang, but it is nowhere near as pronounced as Megan's "Heyyy yawwwwl" that is now burned in my brain. Five years of being in the same class at the same small school will do that to you.

I smiled and nodded, all the while wishing my problems were as simple as "Should I let my 6-year-old have a 'surfer like' haircut?"

She had to cut our coffee date short so she could prep for her speech. Did I mention Megan was perfect? Before she left, she floated the idea of getting together the following evening. She explained the conference would end Friday but she wouldn't fly out until midday Saturday. I already knew Keira was busy with her daughter, and I wasn't making plans with Jacob these days, so I agreed to meet Megan for apps and drinks at a local seafood restaurant.

When I arrived and saw Megan at the restaurant, she seemed looser, more let down. Her blonde beach waves flowed past her shoulders, a drastic difference from the slick bun she wore the day before. Her bright red lips, visible cleavage, and miniskirt were a stark contrast to the pinstripe business suit she had been rocking when we met for coffee. She was already a couple drinks in when I arrived.

Megan acknowledged my presence with an enthusiastic "HILLLLLL!" She slammed her drink down causing a little to splash out of her glass and reached out to hug me. She lingered long enough that I could tell she was feeling that Mai Tai.

 "Great, now I have to babysit a grown ass woman who can't handle her liquor," I thought, rolling my eyes.

"I'm soooooooo glad you're here." She said, pulling away and returning to her seat.

"Awww, thanks. I'm glad to be here." I said, because we southern women are nothing if not polite.

Somehow we managed to bullshit our way through four rounds of drinks. Me talking about my article and her raving about her kids. She really did seem like a great mom. Right after the server asked us if we were ready to order and we realized we hadn't even looked at the menu, Megan looked at me intently.

"You wanna get outta here?" She asked. Her southern drawl caused each syllable to last a little longer than it should.

"Sure." I replied, totally unsure if I wanted to continue hanging out with her.

We ended up back at her hotel, where she cracked open a bottle of Pinot Noir and started spilling her guts. She confessed that she wasn't happy in her relationship, though she loved her kids, she mostly hated being a mother, she was under constant pressure at home, work, and church. Through tears, she lamented, "They all expect me to be 100% theirs at all times and I have no time for me. None! This conference is the first time I've been alone for longer than a 2-hour stretch in five years. Five YEARS!" She cried. She confessed that her marriage was basically over, but she feared divorce.

"How would I ever recover from letting down my family, and God by leaving my husband?" She lamented.

This was the first time I saw Megan as anything less than perfect, yet her imperfection made her even more endearing. Dare I say, more perfect. She was like a caged bird finally able to spread her wings thanks to her husband's desire to save some money. "It's cheaper to just stay at the hotel another night, as long as you don't spend more than $50.00 on food." Her husband, who was the "head of house-hold", made all the financial decisions. He decided she would stay in New Orleans another night, and gave her a strict spending limit for her extra day, which was why she was so drunk. She hadn't eaten anything all day so she would have money to spend that night. This was the first time Megan felt a sense of freedom, and she was going to take full advantage of her extra night.

I opened up to her a little, but not fully, because even though she had just been so vulnerable with me, I couldn't trust her enough to tell her my truth. But man, I was dying to. Or at least, someone aside from Jill. I wanted to trust someone without buying their silence. (Thank you, HIPAA laws). I did tell Megan that things weren't great in my marriage, and even though Theo and I loved each other very much, we weren't sure we could make it work.

Before I finished explaining what I was willing to divulge about my marriage, she wrapped her arms around me and started kissing me. It took my brain a minute to process what was happening, as this was completely unexpected. Megan was kissing me. Megan, the perfect Christian. Megan, a woman. I was kissing a woman? Her lips were so soft, and to my surprise, her lipstick didn't taste like anything. Before my brain could fully register what was happening her hands were on my waist and a rush of electricity coursed through my veins. I came to my senses and pushed her away.

"What are you doing?" I asked, sounding more upset than intrigued, even though I felt more of the latter.

"I'm sorry... I just... I ... it's. I never get to do anything I want to do." She struggled to give words to her feelings.

"And what do you want to do?" I asked as I leaned in to kiss her again.

"I think." She said between kisses. "I want to do this." She told me as she slipped her hands under my shirt.

I really liked making out with her, but I couldn't quite get over the fact that I was kissing a female. In terms of evangelical sins, this was almost as bad as getting an abortion. My long-held beliefs that same-sex relationships were sinful fell away in an instant, even though it had been a long time coming. I was fine. This was okay. My tongue was in a woman's mouth and all I kept thinking was how not different it was. Kissing felt like kissing.

"I'm not a lesbian," she told me, definitively.

"Me neither," I said, while kissing her neck.

Having sex with women was an idea Theo touted back in Austin, just before I left. He said even though he was fine with whatever I want to do, he loved the idea of me being with a woman.

"I just think you'll like it. Women are prettier, softer than guys. It will be such a different experience for you, and something you've never been allowed to even consider," Theo told me one night as we lay in bed. His patience and openness helped me so much over the years, but I still had a long way to go.

After a mildly awkward, really intense makeout session, I looked over at Megan, who had fallen asleep, and thought maybe, just maybe, I've gained some ground. The familiar feeling of shame showed up shortly after though. I went into the bathroom and cried. Did I just sin? Does God hate me? Once again, I didn't really feel bad, but my conditioning started to get the best of me.

"I am a grown woman. I had above the belt physical contact with someone who initiated it. It felt good. She is in charge of her relationships, not me. I do not know the inner workings of her marriage. I am not a homewrecker or a whore or a sinner, and I have nothing to regret." In order to help squelch the negative self-talk filling my mind, I repeated those words over and over again to the person staring back at me in the mirror. Her approval, her acceptance, was what I needed most.

I contemplated spending the night, but I really wanted to be home. I gathered my things and quietly left. I texted her later, "I'm glad we could meet up. Had a great time. Hope you have a safe flight home! Text me when you land."

She replied, "Same here and will do!"

Megan texted me that she made it home safely, and we didn't talk again until Christmas.

First thing the next morning, I texted Keira. "When is the next time Quinn is with her dad?"

"She's there now. I don't pick her up until tomorrow night." She replied.

"Wanna have a slumber party at my house tonight?" I asked. I couldn't keep this to myself. I had to tell Keira at least some of what was going on in my life.

I went home, showered, napped and prepped for the sleepover. We were going to have a classic girls' night in. I went to the grocery store for Margarita mix and chips and queso before cleaning up my place and putting on Dirty Dancing, one of the movies I was forbidden to watch as a child.

Then, Keira showed up with some more edibles and all my plans for the night went out the window.

Chapter Thirteen

MOST FASCINATED

"Oh my gosh, I'm really high." I told Keira. She giggled, implying that she was too.

We went straight to the heavy stuff, wondering if God was actually the way he is portrayed in the bible and if so, the Old Testament God or the New Testament one? We were questioning the possibility of God not being all knowing, and humans being some sort of divine experiment when I suddenly began divulging everything.

I told her in depth about my strict evangelical upbringing and the way my desire to achieve an unattainable purity had damaged me to my core. I confessed the real reason I was in New Orleans, explaining that even though I was sleeping with other people, it was my attempt at healing myself for Theo. I told her what happened with Jacob in Franklinton and what happened with Megan the night before. I know I was high, so that may have been part of it, but I poured out this deeply personal information matter-of-factly. I had feelings about it all, sure, but when I was talking to Keira, my words were devoid of any real emotion.

After processing everything I had dumped on her, Keira was most fascinated, a little perturbed even, with the fact that I had kissed a girl. She questioned me intensely.

"Was it different? How did it make you feel?"

"No...maybe? A little? I don't know. Not...significantly different. I feel okay about it now. At first, I was worried I was going to be struck by lightning." I confessed.

"Does this mean you're bisexual?" Keira wondered aloud.

"I don't know... Does the fact that I didn't hate making out with a girl make me bi?" I answered as honestly as possible, but I had no idea what anything meant at the time.

"Would you... Do it again?" Keira asked. We looked at each other in a way we had looked at each other before, but this time, we didn't look away. We leaned in to the rush of emotions and our lips met. Keira reached her hand out and gently caressed my cheek. "You are an incredible woman." She told me.

"So are you." I replied.

Our connection was strong, but until this point, our relationship had never gotten physical. I thought I felt a hint of sexual tension between us, but I suppressed it. Kissing her and touching her body felt so right. As if this is what our friendship had been missing.

Her soft lips. Her long hair. Her beautiful, lickable breasts. The firm way her tongue met mine. The taste of her chapstick. Her delicate hands on the small of my back.

We spent hours exploring each other's bodies. I looked up to watch her arch her back and lift her neck as her thighs trembled in my hands. I didn't know one night could produce so many orgasms.

Megan opened the door to something I'd wanted with Keira all along.

"I'm think I'm a lesbian." She confessed a while later, when I was half asleep. "Well, maybe not." She continued. "But I'm at least 50% gay."

"Based on your performance, I think you are too," I teased. After I let out a post-sex-tired yawn, I asked Keira if she was okay with me not identifying as a lesbian, or even bisexual. At that point in my life, I was resistant to labels.

"No. I knew you weren't. I just, since you opened up about your life and what you were doing here, I figured why not take a chance. I've always thought you were hot, but figured you were off limits. I was honestly afraid to tell you I like being with women as much as, maybe more than, I like being with men."

"I'm sorry I didn't make you feel safe to tell me that before," I told her.

"Oh, no. It's not you. I'm just navigating these muddy waters," she replied. She went on to tell me how hard it is to navigate life with an ex who was for *traditional* marriage. For her, coming out as bisexual or a lesbian could cause problems with her ex-in-laws, affecting not only her life, but her daughter's as well.

I was so angry for her that she couldn't be herself. Of course, I couldn't be myself either, at least, not my current self around my church community. For a group that preaches unconditional love, Evangelicalism sets very clear conditions.

Keira was the only person aside from Theo (and my therapist) who knew what I was doing. I worried adding sex, even great sex, into the mix would mess things up between us, but we were lucky. Over the next several weeks, we almost seamlessly toed the line between friends and lovers. My affection for her was unrestricted. She was free to do whatever she wanted with whomever she wanted, and so was I. There was little to no jealousy between us. When we were together, we were into one another wholly, yet we did not have any constraints around our relationship. We were, essentially, in a non-monogamous relationship. She had other lovers, as did I, but in New Orleans, we had each other, first and foremost. I will be forever grateful for that time, because we needed each other more than we originally realized. The universe knew what she was doing when she brought Keira and I together.

Chapter Fourteen

DRASTIC MEASURES

"WE JUST DON'T KNOW HOW TO COMMUNICATE," I TOLD OUR therapist, hot tears streaming down my face.

"I don't understand why she's so emotional," Theo replied.

Theo and I had been in therapy almost our entire marriage, but a few months before I moved, we started meeting with a new, younger therapist.

"I can tell you right now, you're going to have to resort to drastic measures if you want to save your marriage. But I'm confident you can do it."

Betsy, 26 and straight out of school, was either incredibly naïve or brilliant beyond her years for thinking Theo and I had a chance.

Life was so hard then. We were two very different people, broken in very different ways, seeking healing from one another when neither of us were capable of helping the other.

If I hadn't grown up Christian, we'd probably be divorced. I'm sure Theo had considered divorce. We had become so disconnected, even though we loved each other immensely. We were great partners, but we weren't great lovers. We weren't even good lovers. I couldn't understand sex. I didn't know I was allowed to enjoy it. I didn't know how good it could feel because I didn't know how to relax. I was ashamed of my nakedness, my sexuality, and sensuality. I couldn't be myself in bed. Even after I moved away from my faith, I still couldn't get comfortable with sex. I'm honestly surprised Theo didn't give up on me, on us.

"I believe if you want to, you can fix this. You can heal yourselves while holding space for each other to grow and stumble. Life is hard. Marriage is hard. But y'all can do hard things," Betsy assured us.

She gave us some unorthodox advice, like pressing pause during arguments. She said taking a time out to have sex while we were in the middle of an argument could be good for us.

When we spoke privately, she encouraged me to see my sexuality as a gift, explaining that my body wasn't a temptation or a stumbling block. She had so much insight to offer, especially since she had only been a practicing therapist for about a year. Betsy was the one who floated the idea of an open marriage.

"It's too bad you can't have a do-over. One where you made space for your sexual desires and where having sex for fun was allowed. I bet if you could live a hedonistic lifestyle for a little bit, your intimacy problems, which seem to be the root of most of your marital struggles, would all but disappear." She told me during one of our sessions.

Initially, I didn't consider that a real possibility. Only a "too bad we can't."

At the time, I was surprised Theo was still with me. Before we were married, when we weren't having sex, I was able to be more myself. Once I took on the role of wife, I began to unravel. The insecurity and shame I had come to live with led to a diagnosis of Generalized Anxiety Disorder. Theo had the patience of a saint. Delving into my past made me realize the extent of my shame and self-loathing around sex and sexuality, which brought tremendous feelings of guilt. "The problems in your marriage are all your fault," my mind would tell me. Even though I had moved away from Evan-gelical Christianity in practice, its views on men, women, and sex continued to torment me.

I would do anything to heal and save my marriage. I didn't understand how this could be happening to me, a person who did all the right things. Was a failing marriage my reward for going out of my way to not tempt boys with my body and breaking up with guys I liked too much?

Seeing a non-Christian therapist was the first time I got a glimpse how traumatic my past had been. Initially, I was hesitant to call it trauma. I wasn't physically or sexually abused. My parents were married. Though conservative, my parents were shockingly progressive in some ways. In a time when working outside the home was still uncommon in the church, my mom worked as an emergency dispatcher and my dad helped with some of the domestic responsibilities. Did my church leaders know they were traumatizing me? Was the subordination and objectification of women delib-erate? My struggles weren't strictly about the huge emphasis they put on purity for girls, but that was the single biggest reason my marriage was falling apart. Even in the confines of marriage, I struggled to see myself as pure or worthy. They likened girls who had sex to a wilted rose, tattered wrapping paper, chewed gum, a half-eaten cookie, or some other dehumanizing metaphor for used up and worthless.

Betsy sat in dismay as I recounted the church's teachings on female virginity during a solo session.

"You are a goddess, Hillary. Your sexuality is yours alone. You were lied to," she told me. She continued, "Did you know the female orgasm has no purpose?"

"Wh....what do you mean?" I struggled to speak, still uncomfortable with the word orgasm.

"Unlike the male orgasm, which is necessary for procreation" she said with authority, "the female orgasm is simply for pleasure. Why would your God equip you like this if he didn't want you to enjoy sex?"

Betsy was so forward-thinking. I had never been taught anything about my body, and I finally felt like I was on the right track.

In fact, it only took a few sessions with Betsy for Theo to up his resolve to save our marriage. We started talking extensively about the nature of my upbringing and how much it damaged me. I had spent so much time convincing myself that I was okay when I wasn't. I was treated like a possession, belonging to my father until one day, I grew up and became my husband's possession. This messaging told me my worthiness lived in my vagina and could be taken if I got too close to sexual impurity. We talked about all the ways in which purity culture skewed my thinking.

Those first few sessions with Betsy were the beginning of what would forever change my life, my marriage and my faith.

Chapter Fifteen

SEXUAL IMPURITY

"What does the term 'sexual impurity' even mean?" I asked.

"I have no idea." Jacob replied, seeming unmoved by the seriousness of the question.

We were in high school when we had that conversation, and at the time, we were receiving far different messages about sexual purity and impurity. Jacob was taught to stay a virgin until he got married, and that his feelings of sexual desire were wrong, while I was busy trying to navigate the increasingly rigid expectations to remain pure for my future husband.

After a particularly heavy makeout session, which I pumped the brakes on, I lifted my head from his chest and softly asked, "Do you think we'll get married someday?"

"I hope so, babe. You'll make an amazing wife." Jacob told me.

"What did he mean by that?" I asked Jill during our August

29th session. I remember the date clearly because it was the anniversary of Hurricane Katrina, and all the local news outlets were covering the story. "Was it because he loved me or because I was playing the role of the good Christian girl who was going to grow up to be a good Christian wife?"

"Only he can answer that." She told me, giving me no indication as to whether or not I should ask him.

"I just... I know we loved each other. And I can't tell if we broke up for the wrong reasons. I never thought about it much before, but being here and feeling freer than I ever have, I can't help but wonder if we are being given a second chance. Am I supposed to explore these feelings?"

"As a grown woman, living life on your own terms, you are not 'supposed to' do anything," she told me, air quoting the words supposed to.

"Do you really think I can do whatever I want about Jacob?" I asked for her opinion, but what I was really looking for was permission.

"I think you still don't believe you are the one in charge of your life."

She wasn't one to mince words. Jill was my favorite therapist ever. Betsy was great and had laid the groundwork, but I had such a great rapport with Jill.

My head sunk into my shoulders. She was right. Undoing the teachings of my adolescence was proving to be more difficult than I imagined. I had been under the impression that taking ownership of my body and my physical desires would heal me, and while that was helping, I had so much more to unpack.

I had a very low sense of self, I wasn't a whole person. I was a child of God and of my parents. I was a wife. I wanted to be a mother. But who was I, outside of those around me? That's what I was beginning to explore during my time in New Orleans.

I hadn't talked to Jacob in a few weeks. I don't know if he was a central role in my therapy sessions because of who he was or because he was a tangible representation of my childhood. He was my first love, my first kiss, my first heartbreak. He was the center of my prayers throughout most of high school.

"Dear God, please let Jacob be the one for me."

"Dear God, help me control myself around Jacob."

"Dear God, let Jacob continue to walk with you."

"Dear God, help Jacob get over me, and Lord, do bring him back to me if he's the one."

"Let's talk about you, Hillary. What do you want from your life?" Jill asked me.

"I... I don't know. I want to save my marriage."

"You can't save your marriage until you can fully exist as a whole person outside of it. Based on your experiences since you've been here, you are more sexually free than 90% of my patients. You have accomplished what you set out to accomplish."

"Think about it," she continued, "You hooked up with a guy your first week in town. You slept with, what, three men and a woman in the last three months. Trust me, you've made up for lost time. I've only had sex with four people my entire life and I feel perfectly content in my sexuality!" Jill's ability to be real with me was more helpful than she realized.

"The question isn't, 'Are you free, sexually?' it's, 'Are you a complete person who doesn't need permission from anyone else to go after her dreams?' What are your dreams, Hillary?"

"I want to be a writer," I admitted.

"You are a writer," She quipped.

"No, no. I write for other publications. I love it, and it allows me to be here on assignment right now, but this isn't the kind of writing I want to do."

"Go on." Jill instructed.

"I want to write a book. Well, lots of books. I want to write fiction and nonfiction, or maybe a combination of both. I have an idea for a self-help book and one for a memoir, and I have all sorts of fiction ideas, but I've never written fiction, so we'll see. Basically, I want to use my words to help others live their best life. I want to be my own version of Brené Brown or Elizabeth Gilbert."

"The woman who did Eat Pray Love?" Jill cocked her eyebrows. "I never did like that book. I mean, good for her, it's a nice story and all, but tell me how you found yourself and your healing without traversing the world for a year." She went on to point out the privileged nature of the book, a privilege of which the vast majority of women in the world do not have.

"Soooooo, telling my story about my journey to New Orleans would be a bad idea then? Not relatable?" I said it jokingly, but I really wanted her to answer me. I wanted a roadmap. Someone to tell me what to do to get whole. Do I write books? I know I'm privileged to be able to take this journey; that doesn't mean I need it any less than someone who can't escape their life for a period. I truly hope to one day be able to help people who struggle the way I struggle.

May the pain of my heart and the privilege of my experience help others heal.

Chapter Sixteen

THEO'S VISIT

"ARE YOU SURE YOU WANT TO DO THIS?" KEIRA ASKED ME FOR the third time.

"I'm sure." I replied.

"Once you do it, you won't be able to undo it. This isn't like the movies where two friends get into hijinks by opening a post office mailbox trying to retrieve a letter they regretted sending."

"Stop being so dramatic, Keira. I want this. I'm sure of it." I told her playfully, but I was serious. I knew what I wanted.

I am not sure how to define my relationship with Keira exactly. I was still exploring, and at this point, quite enjoying my sexual liberation, but she was the only person I had sex with *and* hung out with, so that made us dating. Kinda. I think. What can I say? It was a very confusing time.

One thing that was missing from our relationship was jealousy. Not one ounce of jealousy about anything. We could be intimate one minute and the next minute, she'd tell me about her upcoming date or I'd start talking to her about my relationship with Theo. In fact, I was telling her how much I missed Theo when the idea was born.

"Theo hasn't seen me like this, you know?" I told her. I don't know if the great sex was building our friendship or if I felt more vulnerable with her because I was the most sexually open with her or what, but there I was, sharing more of my heart than I normally would.

"Theo only knows me as a shy, timid girl in bed," I continued as we walked through the door of my shotgun double. "I would always make sure he enjoyed himself, and it was pleasurable for me after a few months of wonky sex, but I was always pretty reserved. I laid there like a log, unsure of what I should do. Despite his repeated attempts to show me, I couldn't believe that my feelings mattered. He seemed satisfied with our sex life, but I convinced myself he wanted more. I didn't know how to give him more." I hung my head in embarrassment. "No one told me I could enjoy sex, too."

Keira responded with a warm, reassuring hug that helped heal my hurting heart, just a bit.

"In just a couple months you'll be able to show him who you are and all the dirty things you're capable of," she whispered in my ear, turning me from cold to hot in 22 words.

"I don't want to wait. I want to show him now," I told her as I twirled her hair between my fingers.

She leaned in closer.

"I bet he'd love to see us together," I whispered into her ear.

Keira reached around my waist to pull my shirt over my

head, leaving me standing in my pink bra and jeans. Immediately her shirt joined mine on the floor. She got close to me and pulled on my bra strap then said, "Why don't we let him."

Unexpected shockwaves pulsed through my body at the thought of having Keira and Theo at the same time.

While I had experimented more sexually in the last few months than I had my entire life, I never seriously considered a threesome. After Keira and I started having sex, though, things really began to change within me. The idea of kissing two of my favorite people at the same time filled me with excitement. I knew if I didn't seize this moment, I'd never have another chance. Together, Keira and I hatched a plan.

First, we would make a teaser video of an erotic fantasy, like a role playing thing. Keira dressed like a police officer, with her cleavage popping out of her tiny blue sexy-cop costume, and I had on a bright orange button down mini-dress and handcuffs. We got footage of her sensually frisking me, running her hands up and down my body, feeling every crevice. After edits and a little cinematic flair, we mailed Theo what can only be described as a porn trailer starring the two of us, along with the name of a hotel we booked for the following weekend and the following letter:

Dear Theo,

Your wife has been very naughty. She was getting away with it for a while, but her antics have caught up to her. She's been placed under house arrest and I'm taking very good care of her, but if she is to go free, we're going to need you to come bail her out.

Officer McHottie

The idea was he'd either fly in and we would all three spend the night together, or he wouldn't and Keira and I would have a hotel room for three straight days. It was win/win.

The Saturday of the event, Keira and I had checked into the hotel. We were fully in character and into our third glass of wine when we heard a knock at the door. I confirmed through the peephole that it was Theo, took a deep breath and motioned for Keira to open the door.

"Are you Officer McHottie?" he asked Keira while he surveyed the room.

"I am," she said with authority. "Your wife, Melody (because if we were role playing, I wanted a character name) has been gallivanting around town with this body wantonly on display. Men and women alike have been losing their minds with lust."

She walked over to me and stroked my arm, from my shoulder all the way to my wrist.

"I had to handcuff her and get her off the street, not just for the town's safety, but her own."

"What do you mean, her own?" Theo asked. When he did, I knew he was all in with the game.

"Look at her." Keira said loudly.

"Look at these curves." She said as she rubbed her hands along my hips. She unbuttoned a few of my buttons, exposing nearly all of my bra.

"And have you seen her rear end?" She turned me around,

lifted my skirt to expose my white cotton panties and gave me a firm smack on the ass.

"It's enough to drive someone wild, don't you think?"

"Definitely," Theo said. He looked at me so intently I almost broke character.

"I'm fine to go out there," I said, wriggling my arm away from Keira, who had linked hers with mine.

I sauntered toward Theo, my hands still cuffed behind my back. I stood just in front of him saying, "You'd be able to control yourself around me, wouldn't you?"

He looked at me in my eyes, then down at my mostly exposed chest, pressed his body against mine and said, "I don't know. I'm having a hard time resisting you right now."

"See. There's lust everywhere. I might have to handcuff you too, just to keep you two from losing control and having sex right in front of me."

"What's wrong with losing a little control, Officer McHottie?" I asked, eyeing Keira up and down.

"I... I don't know, but it's against the law and you two are going to be punished." Keira stammered hastily.

"So. Punish us." I said defiantly, as I kissed Theo. He placed his hands on my dress and began unbuttoning it. He continued kissing me, moving from my mouth to my neck to my breasts to my stomach. He kept moving further down when Keira interrupted saying,

"This is why I placed you under house arrest. I knew you couldn't be in the presence of a man without it turning sexy."

"What's wrong with sexy?" Theo asked, pushing my now completely unbuttoned dress off my shoulders, fully exposing my bra and panties.

"I don't know what's wrong but it feels wrong," she protested.

"I think," I said just before I kissed her lips, "you'll enjoy it." She kissed me back.

I pushed my nearly naked body as close to her as possible, my handcuffs keeping me somewhat constrained.

"Why don't you just relax, Officer McHottie," Theo suggested as he walked up behind her and started massaging her shoulders.

Keira enjoyed it for a second then pulled away. "Oh, you're worse than she is, aren't you?" She grinned. She reached behind my back and uncuffed me. "It looks like you need these more than your wife does."

She stroked Theo's arms, bringing them around to the back and clicked the handcuffs around his wrists.

Keira pushed Theo down to the bed. She lowered her chest toward his face and asked, "Why are you two so obsessed with having sex?"

"We're not. You are," I said, as I moved toward her. I began unbuttoning her fitted, navy police uniform top while I kissed her neck.

"You're the one who won't stop talking about it. I think you want it more than we do." I worked my way down her chest, kissing the skin around her black polka-dot bra.

"Oh, I don't know," she said seductively. "It looks like he

wants it more than both of us." She motioned to Theo who was entranced by our performance.

"I know what he wants." I said as I removed the rest of Keira's uniform, leaving us both in our underclothes. "He wants to watch. Don't ya babe?" I said just before I started kissing Keira.

Keira and I joined Theo on the bed where we kept him handcuffed for a little while, kissing him and rubbing him top to bottom. Keira eventually reached her mostly naked body around his back to remove the handcuffs and they started heavily making out. Seeing two people I was sexually attracted to enjoy each other was one of the biggest turn ons of my life. The room got hotter by the minute as we let go of any and all inhibitions. After what can only be described as us exploding with pleasure, the three of us fell asleep together. By the time Keira and I woke up the next morning, Theo was gone.

Chapter Seventeen

THESE MEMORIES

WHO EVEN AM I? I WROTE IN MY JOURNAL. I STARTED KEEPING one when I was twelve, and being able to process my thoughts and feelings through writing has saved me on more than one occasion.

Purity culture caused me to walk a fine line between two different and competing beliefs about sex and sexuality. Before marriage, I had to repress all of my sexuality, but once I became a wife, I had to become a sex goddess for my husband's pleasure. However, I still could not exude any sort of sexuality outside of my home. I got the message that they wanted me to dress and act as asexually as possible until it was time to strip off my clothes and perform for my husband. It wasn't enough for me to stay a virgin until I was married. I had to then transform into a sexpot for my husband. Where was I in all this teaching? According to my church, I could hinder my spiritual growth by being too sexual before marriage or by having sex outside of my marriage, and inside the marriage, my actions or lack of could hinder my husband's growth by making him susceptible to sexual temptation. My wants, needs or desires were never mentioned. I was taught not to consider myself at all when it came to sex.

I want to believe everything happens for a reason, but if I could go back, I would change so many things. I would never have let the people charged with raising me and teaching me about the love of God tell me I didn't matter. I matter, dammit. How much time did I waste? Would I have finished college? Would I have stayed with Jacob? Would I have even dated Jacob in the first place?

I know who the church thinks I am. They think I'm a "troubled" girl because my family was one of the poorest families in the church. Sure, I was a little rough around the edges, but my desire for God burned strong. I wasn't like the "good girls" who got the lead roles in the church plays; the ones constantly called up to give their testimonies, who received incessant praise simply because their looks fit the narrative of either the reformed sinner or the saintliest saint. I did not fit the mold, but my unwavering faith was noticed by the youth pastor who asked me to be a youth leader. My fervor increased with my newfound responsibility. I wanted to honor God and help others, and youth leadership would allow me to do both. Sadly, I was let down. The leadership meetings were a combination of pissing contests between the guys and some uncomfortable flirting between the married youth pastor and one of the too-old-for-youth-group female leaders.

All these memories, which I didn't know I had, came flooding back while I was in New Orleans. I recalled my youth group experience, including the rumors that flew about the youth pastor sexually assaulting one of the teen girls, and the victim in question being shunned from the church for trying to speak out. I still don't know the entire story, but a once well known, well liked girl who was close to the youth pastor's wife suddenly left the church. I didn't even hear the rumor until months later, but looking back, all the evidence pointed to its validity. Yet *I* am the one my church community would judge if they knew about my current life.

Why are so many Evangelicals obsessed with sex, anyway? It becomes a self-fulfilling prophecy. They obsess over sex and view everything through a sexualized lens, then they are offended everything seems over-sexualized. My friend's husband didn't allow Victoria's Secret magazines in their house. That said a lot more about his pent up sexual desires than it did about the women wearing swimsuits and underwear.

My evangelical roots ran so deep that even though I had moved away from my church's teachings, I spent the first year or so of our relationship being jealous of Theo's female coworkers, worried he would be "led into temptation" by them. I couldn't help but wonder, as I reflected, if Christian women saw me like that? When I worked on a project with a married man, was I viewed as someone who could lead him astray? How on earth could I have that much power? Was I a witch? Was my sensual body draped in normal, modest clothing too much for married men to handle?

Once, during my youth leadership days, there was a short-lived rumor that I was tempting David, the worship leader's fiancé, with my female anatomy, the same anatomy that every other female in the world had. Was I that difficult to resist? Is that why that douchebag made a pass at me when I was working with him on a writing assignment about the music ministry? Am I that much of a seductress? My disdain for David must have been hard to recognize since I did my best to act professionally when we had to work together. The respect I try to show all humans comes across as burning lust for all the married men. It's as if my standing up to leave the room was actually a ploy to put my ass within grabbing distance of David's hand. It *obviously* wasn't his fault. Men cannot be held accountable for their illegal and immoral actions when there are women walking around with breasts and hips. Men are only doing what we women summon them to do, right?

When it happened, I wanted to put it out of my mind as quickly as possible. He thought he was entitled to do what he wanted to my body simply because I shared space with him. Fuck that. Fuck all of the so-called Christians who allow such behavior from Christian men who think women are there for their pleasure, rather than recognizing our equal standing in this world; that man came from a woman, as all men do. It is high time women claim our rightful seat at the table.

Chapter Eighteen

LATE SEPTEMBER

"Hillary?" I heard a semi-sure voice say right after I took a giant bite of my burger.

I chewed as fast as I could and quickly grabbed a sip of my water. "Oh my gosh, hi!!" I squealed, hoping he would say his name because of course I knew he was the notary from Sean's house.

Though it was still hot and muggy out, I decided to grab dinner at a patio restaurant and eat outside that late September evening. I was heading home from the library. I looked like crap, which back in Austin would mean I was likely to run into someone I knew, but I figured I was safe from such a fate in New Orleans, having still been new in town, but I underestimated the smallness of the city.

"It's me, Jose, from Sean's house, remember?" he said.

"Of course, of course! How are things?"

We exchanged pleasantries until the cashier called him to

come pick up his cheeseburger and onion rings. Just before he walked out, he turned back and said, "I'm meeting up with Sean and some friends later, wanna join us?"

"Maybe... I'm pretty tired, but I'll try." I said, attempting to play it cool.

I scarfed down my food, raced home and made myself up to look like I hardly did anything to get ready, donning a pair of cute jeans, black high heels, a comfy-but-casual sexy cotton t-shirt, and a new pair of underwear. In keeping with the messy-but-hot look I chose the cotton boy-short panties. I took my hair out from my bun, gave it a quick tousle and headed out the door.

I had no idea if Sean was still dating the barista's sister or what, but if he was single, I really wanted to make one of my many fantasies about him come to life.

"Moxie!" Sean shouted from across the room, opening his arms. My heels clanked across the floor as I hurried toward him to greet him with a tight hug.

"It's so good to see you!" I told him. I meant it, not just in an obligatory way. Even though this is a small town, I don't see too many of the same people. Plus, I wanted to have dirty dirty sex with him.

"How's the car?" He shouted over the music. I laughed and motioned for him to come sit in the courtyard. We sat down at one of the high top tables, where I told him how helpful the little black civic had been, and about my research gathering for my story. I also made some corny jokes because that's what I do when I'm nervous. I wanted to ask him if he was seeing anyone. I didn't want to make him uncomfortable if he was unavailable, but I really wanted him and had to find out if there was even a chance for us.

Instead of strategically working it into the conversation, I blurted out, "So, are you still seeing the girl you were dating when we first met?"

"Nope," he replied with a knowing grin.

During the next couple of hours, the sexual tension between Sean and me became so thick you could cut it with a knife. During a game of darts, he stood close behind me, so close I could feel his breath on the back of my neck. He placed one hand on my hip. He held his other hand over my hand. He said, "Let me show you how it's done."

I turned back to face him, nearly touching his lips with mine and replied, "I know how to do it," before hurling the dart toward the bullseye. I missed, but it was close. He asked me if I wanted to get out of there, and just then I remembered Megan asking me the very same thing.

"Of course," I replied. Unlike with Megan, I knew exactly what was coming, and I was looking forward to it.

When we got back to his place we had a beer at his kitchen table, just like we did a month or so earlier. When I was halfway finished with my beer and we had just wrapped up a conversation about women's rights, I got up from my chair and walked over to him. I turned his body toward mine, spread his knees apart, and straddled him. Without a moment's hesitation, I leaned in and kissed him. He grabbed my hips, stood up from the chair, and carried me to his bedroom, kissing me the whole way. His hands, like his movements, were strong. He was dominating, but not domineering. He touched me firmly but lovingly, his dark hands a sharp and beautiful contrast to my pale stomach. Everything felt so good that it started to feel wrong, but feeling wrong made it feel even better and made me want him even more until finally, I couldn't take it anymore and begged him to fuck me. I had never said that out loud before, but I couldn't help it. Sex with Sean reminded me of the vinegar and baking soda experiment where the pressure from the two chemicals builds and builds until it explodes wildly.

I rested my head on the pillow and faced Sean, who was fast asleep. I wanted to sleep but I was deep in thought. Sometimes my thoughts feel bigger than me, and my night with Sean was one of those times. For a woman who was technically committing a version of adultery, I felt close to the divine. My fantasy had come true, and a little part of me believed I had something to do with making it happen. Why did I go to that particular restaurant on that particular evening? It seemed random, yet there I was, doing exactly what I had envisioned doing so many times in so many ways over the last five weeks. And it wasn't about the sex, which was mind blowing, but the beautiful mystery of this life.

The next morning Sean made us coffee and breakfast, and we chatted until almost noon. I loved his stories. Having sex with him was fantastic, but I was starting to realize the orgasm itself wasn't any better than in my fantasies. More intense, maybe. One of the things that made me enjoy it so much was I liked Sean a lot. He was one of the few people I had met who could dive deep into conversation with me without needing to come up for air.

Before coming to NOLA, I didn't set myself up with any moral or ethical code of conduct aside from, "only have sex with people who want to have sex with me" and "no sex with people in monogamous relationships." But now I was faced with a dilemma I hadn't considered. Sean and his mom were rescued off their 9th Ward rooftop by helicopter following Hurricane Katrina, and I wanted to include him in my story.

Chapter Nineteen

ALWAYS SAVED

"I'm telling you, she's legit."

Iris, the woman who owned and often worked at the convenience store near my shotgun double, had been encouraging me to go see her psychic. Thanks to the friendly nature of the people of New Orleans and my disdain for cooking, I spent quite a bit of time perusing the aisles of the convenience store near my house.

"You look lost, my dear," she would often say to me. Iris was in her late 50's, with two grown children and a grandchild on the way. She was gentle in a way that only comes through hardship. Lines of wisdom graced her face, and she had a kindness in her eyes I don't see very often. In a lot of ways, she reminded me of my own mother. Except my mom would think a psychic was a charlatan at best, and at worst, a demonic spirit. Personally, I just figured a psychic was someone good at reading people and telling them what they want to hear. I have since learned that I was sorely mistaken.

"That's not really my thing," I would tell her. "I'll find myself without anyone else's help." One afternoon, she challenged my answer.

"Connecting with a higher power isn't your thing?" she asked, pointedly. I know she didn't mean offense, but I was hurt by her retort. I'd been trying my entire life to connect with a higher power. I often repeated what's known as the Sinner's Prayer so I could be sure I was saved. My church told me I was "once saved, always saved" out of one side of their mouth while using the other to caution me against the perils of backsliding, a term for not conforming to common Evangelical rules. If anyone from my church had known what I was doing in New Orleans, they would have been discussing how far I'd backslidden. The truth is, I felt closer to God at that time than I did when I was trying to be a good Christian. My thoughts used to be filled with turmoil. After years of feeling like a fraud, I had finally started to feel a relationship with the divine. Iris's question triggered the old feelings of futility from being told that I wasn't seeking God hard enough. At the same time, I was left wondering if I was even a Christian anymore after I considered seeing the psychic, something that was forbidden by the church. I left the store that day fighting back tears.

I spent the evening ugly-crying on my front porch. How could I be closer to God while doing all this sinning? Every-thing I was doing felt so good, so right, yet I still wrestled with guilt. When I got to the end of my tears, peace flowed through me. While swaying back and forth on the swing, I stopped worrying about upsetting God one way or the other. I started believing that God loves me unconditionally, and if I had put myself first to escape the torment of trying to live up to oppressive ideals pushed on me from adolescence, God would understand and support me, not judge and shame me. God was with me, no matter what.

Eventually, my curiosity got the best of me and I gave myself permission to seek the divine in a nontraditional way. I decided to agree to see Iris's psychic the next time I saw her. Only, I never got the chance. That Saturday night, Iris was shot and killed at her store during an attempted robbery.

I wasn't prepared for the level of grief I felt over her death. The tragedy of a life lost, the sadness of seeing someone alive on a Thursday afternoon gone from the world by Sunday morning, the irreplaceable hole her husband and children must now carry in their hearts. The violence. The racial inequity and wealth disparity that fuels the violence. The devastating irony that someone who lived for peace would meet such a violent death, all over a few hundred dollars.

How could God allow this? Who was ultimately responsible here? God? The shooter? Society? The crime in the area of Iris's corner store is directly related to poverty. If our government could pass legislation that would provide resources and paths out of poverty, crime would go down. Why doesn't God put people in charge who care about the least of these?

I believe Iris is in heaven. She loved humans; she cared about me, and I was just a customer. She didn't ask me about my sexual orientation or if I was a sinner in need of a savior. She saw my hurting heart and offered me kindness and nonjudgmental support. I didn't know until the funeral, but year after year she had volunteered as a mentor and donated a portion of her earnings to underserved schools in

New Orleans. Iris was not a Christian, but she was more like Jesus than any pastor or church leader I had ever met, and if the heaven of the Bible exists, she is there. I am embarrassed to admit I used to believe a beautiful soul like Iris would burn in hell because she didn't pray a salvation prayer or ascribe to a specific doctrine.

Her funeral was intimate, yet filled with people whose lives she touched. I kept to myself, sitting near the back and trying to avoid making eye contact with anyone. I wouldn't ordinarily attend the funeral of someone I hardly knew, but she and I shared a connection and I was compelled to pay my respects. As I was ducking out of the funeral home, I heard a familiar phrase directed toward me: "You look lost, my dear." When I turned to see who spoke the words only Iris had said to me before, I saw bold red lips on a striking petite, tan skinned woman wearing a navy peasant top and long black skirt.

"You're the girl on the quest to find herself, aren't you?" Her piercing blue eyes stared into mine as if she knew the answer and was waiting simply for me to confirm.

"I think so. I'm Hillary. I knew Iris from her store." She looked at me intently but said nothing.

"I'm from Austin... I'm here taking a break from my marriage." I tend to ramble when I feel uncomfortable, and the way her eyes surveyed me up and down made me feel like she was peering into the deepest parts of me. That's when I figured out who she was.

"Are you Iris's psychic? Did she tell you about me?"

"I am Talia. And yes, she did." She told me in her Latin

American accent. We talked briefly, sharing memories of Iris before I told her I was on my way out.

"I am too. I'm going to the coffee shop just up the street if you'd like to join me." She extended the invitation in a way that suggested she knew her time was valuable and I should consider myself lucky she was offering to give me any of it.

"Absolutely. I'll meet you there." I said, knowing her time *was* valuable, and I *was* lucky she was offering me any of it.

I arrived first and found us a corner table near the back where we could have some semblance of privacy. When Talia walked in a few minutes later, I offered to get her a coffee. She insisted on paying for her own and selected an herbal tea.

"So, how does this work? Do you just, like, know things about people?" As soon as the words left my lips, I immediately regretted them. I was curious about her work, but I realized my words and tone may have come across disrespectful.

"I'm not here to convince you of my gift. I'm here to share it with you. If you don't want it, we can return our conversation to that of the weather, or I am happy to continue exchanging stories about Iris. She is the reason I am here. Iris came to me in a dream the night she died. She talked to me about many things, and the girl on a quest to find herself was one of them. She wanted me to help you find yourself. If you don't want to talk, I can go."

"No no. I'm sorry." I felt terrible inside. I wanted to know what she knew, or thought she knew. I looked down and stirred my coffee, confessing, "I was hurt by my religion. I'm leery of anyone who says they know something I don't."

"I understand, mija. But there are plenty of differences between me and religious leaders. I believe in many paths to the same destination. I am not going to use my knowledge to tell you how to live your life. I am here for you, but I will not judge you or tell you what to do. I know you are lost. I know you are hurt. I see it all over you." She reached across the table and placed her hand on mine and we sat in silence for a moment. Her hands were warm and soft. I couldn't help but notice the beautiful contrast in our skin tones, and the embarrassing difference in how well we kept up our nails. Hers were long, deep red and freshly manicured, whereas mine were unpainted, short and in desperate need of a nail file.

Returning to our conversation, she said, "You are a special one. I see why Iris wanted me to talk to you."

"Iris always told me I was destined to be here, in New Orleans. I'm flattered she would go through all this trouble to ask you to meet with me." I said. Whether Iris told her at an appointment or from beyond this realm, it was clear she did talk to Talia about me.

"At first, I told her no." She said, unflinching. She could see the confusion on my face. I'm pretty sure if a ghost asked me for a favor I'd say yes, but maybe that's why I'm not a medium.

She continued, "I told Iris I get paid for my gifts. The world would be a much better place if we all got paid for our gifts."

"What do you mean?" I gently inquired as to not offend Talia with my question.

"We focus too much on talents and skills. We all have skills, talents, and gifts. Our gifts, when shared, make the world brighter. Our gifts are how we express ourselves. We should benefit from expressing ourselves to the world."

Her insight caused something to stir inside of me. I did wish we lived in a culture where everyone could be compensated for sharing their gifts with the world. Theo was a graphic designer because of his skills and talents, but music was his gift, his expression.

"Why do you resist the word storyteller?" Talia pointedly asked. I was shocked, as I really did cringe at the word, but hardly ever mentioned that to anyone. I have no recollection of telling Iris about my disdain for the way storyteller had become a buzzword.

"I... I don't know." I stammered. Until that point, I had no idea why I recoiled at the word. "I think because everyone has a story to tell. It's not a term that identifies only some of us. Telling stories, sharing our experiences with others, that's part of being human. I don't like the term being used to separate and elevate some people as if only some of us are storytellers and others aren't. We are all story-tellers."

"Sometimes, the things we dislike can give us a glimpse into our purpose." Talia said, unflinching. "You are a gifted story-teller, and you don't have to be mystic to know that. I could tell by hearing your stories about Iris."

Storytelling was my gift, Talia insisted. She said what I did with the information was up to me, but she saw me as a person who could use stories to help others. She told me I was born to share. To share stories I've lived, witnessed, and learned about. She told me I could write novels and give speeches. She even said she could see me writing a memoir for mothers one day. Tears pooled in my eyes. Her words struck a chord I did not know I had.

"We all have a guide. For some, it's a religious God. Some call it intuition, and others a higher self, and some attribute their guide to nothing more than biology and evolution. A few even believe they can see their guide." She winked at me when she finished her sentence. "Your guide will lead you down the correct path. All you have to do is trust and follow." She told me.

"That sounds a lot like my church. They wanted me to follow Jesus, but instead, imposed a bunch of rules and expectations on me that have nothing to do with him." I said, looking up and blinking quickly in an effort to stop the tears from escaping my eyes.

"Your guide should be gentle with your pain and patient with your growth. A good guide will sit with you when you need a rest and quietly follow you when you attempt a shortcut. You need a guide who helps you when you fall and is free of judgement. A guide who loves you like a mother loves her baby. Your religion was the wrong guide, but the right one is within you." The power in her voice stunned me into silence. I hardly remember the rest of our conversation. Her words replayed in my ears as I could almost feel myself meeting my guide. There was nothing audible or tangible about the experience, but at that little table with Talia, the guide within me awakened.

As we left, I noticed she turned to walk down the street instead of into the parking lot. "Do you need a ride?" I called out.

She replied "No, mija. I only go where my feet can take me."

If life were a movie, she would have disappeared into the fog. In reality, she turned the corner, presumably heading back to her home or studio.

Whether it was before or after her passing, I will be forever grateful to Iris for mentioning me to Talia.

Chapter Twenty

INNER NARRATOR

"WHAT TIME SHOULD I COME OVER?" I TEXTED KEIRA.

The days and weeks were progressing, and I continued working on myself, without sex. I was doing well, at least in the guy department. I stopped checking the dating apps. I kept my communication with Sean, who had become one of my interviewees, mostly to email. The only person I couldn't quit was Keira. We would spend at least two days a week together, usually at her house when Quinn was with her dad. Typically, our evenings involved cooking, reading each other's writings, laughing until we cried, running errands and binge watching TV.

"Actually, can we stay at your place, I didn't get a chance to clean up," she replied.

"Sure, but I don't mind the mess," I insisted. I tried to make her more comfortable with me.

"Regular mess and toddler mess aren't the same, lol." She wouldn't budge.

"I know! I used to babysit. I don't care if you have macaroni and cheese all over your table or random Legos strewn across your floor. You can definitely come here, but I want you to know I'm fine with your mess."

I was trying to help Keira see that I accepted her completely, even her mess. She was so unsure of herself sometimes. I don't think she could believe anyone truly wanted her. I did, though. I had no plans to leave Theo for her, and I was clear about that, but we were both content to live in the moment and not concern ourselves about what the future might bring. She was so easy to talk to. Because her ex-husband grew up in a church similar to mine, she had some under-standing of the messaging I received. We spent the late summer and early fall growing closer as friends and lovers.

While she was at my house one evening, I asked Keira if she thought God was real. I was searching for some sort of sign from God. Something to tell me what to do. I wanted to do the right thing so badly. I knew I was far from the right thing within the Christian framework, but I also knew, despite my sexual openness, my heart was pure. I cared about the "least of these" the church kept telling me I should care about. My church did an excellent job with their homeless ministry, collecting and distributing blankets and food, yet when I would propose policy changes that would genuinely help reduce homelessness, such as expanding the budget for Housing Projects, my Christian friends would grimace and call me a label they thought was inferior and less Christian: Liberal.

"I think God is real, sort of. Not in the Christian sense. Not even in the creator sense. But I feel like we all have a God, an inner narrator to help guide us on our path," Keira told me. Her belief reminded me of my encounter with Talia and her mention of a guide. I was still unpacking everything that happened with her after Iris's funeral. Sometimes I wondered if Talia were a ghost herself, as I couldn't find anything about her on the internet.

"But what about people whose inner narrator tells them to hurt other people?" I asked.

"Not all the narrators are good, I guess," she postulated. "Or maybe we've screwed up humanity for so long we have created some pretty bad seeds."

Keira posed some thought-provoking questions. For so long, I felt like I was a bad Christian, never being able to get it just right. Like Baby Bear's chair, porridge, and bed in the story of Goldilocks, at church everything, including our sin, had to be *just right*.

We could curse, but we couldn't smoke. We could kiss, but we couldn't have sex. We could gossip all day long, no one gave us any crap about that. We could be greedy, but not so greedy that we withheld our tithes and offerings. Giving to the church was seen as noble, and withholding tithes was practically blasphemous. I remember once we had a new member of our church, a young single mom who felt compelled to give her 10% even though she was hardly making ends meet. Instead of the church offering to help her, she got the message that she should give to this million-dollar establishment in order to fit the mold and be accepted. I know, because she confessed one day how messed up it all seemed to her.

"They keep telling me God will be my son's dad; that I shouldn't worry about dating anyone. Well, you know what,

God isn't going to keep my lights on and play football with my son!" she said to a few of us one day after Bible study. At the time, I had nothing better to offer than empty platitudes. I see now that she was crying out for tangible help and practical guidance, not thoughts and prayers.

The church made it clear what was allowed under the "freedom of Christ" they kept telling us we had. We could show mercy, but it stopped short of most forms of sexuality. No mercy for those who fornicated or loved others of the same sex. No mercy for those who felt they were born into the wrong body. No mercy for anyone who strayed from the hetero-norms which had been set up centuries ago. Women were to marry men, ideally of the same race, have children, and that was that. Why did my church care so much about who we loved and what we did with our sexuality?

"What if God doesn't know everything? What if God made us, but he didn't know what we would do when he woke us up and breathed the breath of life into us? What if there are no hard and fast rules?" I pondered my what-if questions with Keira. Rarely did I feel safe to contemplate versions of God that didn't fall in line with evangelical Christianity.

"You don't have to follow their rules. You aren't following their rules." Keira's words gave me strength.

There I was, in bed with a woman, talking about God, Christianity, and my place in the faith. Of course, I knew there was no place for me in my church. Given the choice, I'm sure they would rather me divorce Theo because a sexually free woman posed a much bigger threat to my patriarchal church than a divorced one. I loved God, though. Or at least, Jesus. I didn't know if he was the actual God of the universe or if he was a total lunatic, but his words played through my mind on a loop.

"In everything, do to others what you would have them do to you."

"Love your neighbor as you love yourself."

"Let the one among you who is without sin be the first to cast a stone."

"For what shall it profit a man if he gains the whole world but loses his own soul?"

"Judge not, that you be not judged. For with what judgment you judge, you will be judged; and with the measure you use, it will be measured back to you."

"WHO ARE THEY TO JUDGE ME?!" I shouted.

Keira, sensing my pain, took me into her arms and held me close. My rage turned to tears and I sobbed for the girl I used to be. I cried for that lost child, desperately seeking approval from God, from her church, only to be continually told she wasn't enough. She wasn't pure enough. She wasn't modest enough. She wasn't smart enough, until she was too smart and they all but shunned her from the community she worked so hard to join.

"Do you know what my upbringing was like?" I asked Keira.

"Though I'm paraphrasing, the teachings sounded something like this:

'If you have sex, you will become impure, like a tattered gift, and sure, I mean, God can rebuild you but you'll be forever jacked up, so um, don't do it, okay? Oh, and be sure to wear a shirt over your bathing suit because boys, you know the ones over there, swimming in whatever they feel most comfortable wearing because *their* bodies aren't an issue, those boys might stumble because of yours. So, keep yourself as asexual as possible. Your breasts are bad for boys. Your curves are stumbling blocks for boys. You will be held accountable if a boy chases you, makes a pass at you, gets physical with you and even if he touches you without your consent. You are an evil temptress, a descendant of Eve, the mother of all sin. Do not think about sex. Do not ask about sex. Sex is bad for you. Until you get married, that is. Then everything changes. Married women are to have sex with their husbands whenever he wants. You have to, in order to keep your husband satisfied, otherwise, he might stray. It is the will of God. You are to go from being responsible for boys' purity to being responsible for your husband's satisfaction. Got all that, girls?'"

Tears were streaming down my cheeks as I came face to face with the reality that their teachings had been spiritual abuse.

"I was so much more than my body!!" I slammed my hand down on the bed.

I probably should have saved all this for therapy, but Keira didn't seem to mind. She told me about her ex-husband, Brad, and how he was taught basically that he was nothing but a little horn dog, and to avert his eyes anytime he felt a twinge of sexual desire.

"I didn't know what to do when I found myself aroused at a woman's intelligence." Brad told her once.

"These boys were only taught about the physical attraction of a woman, and that was dangerous. The fact that our minds, our humor, or our passion could be sexy was foreign to them," she continued.

"I'm so glad I met Theo when I did." My tears still flowed, but the reason I was crying changed from frustration with the church to missing my husband.

"He was unlike anyone I ever knew. He grew up in a sex-positive culture, where sex was viewed as wonderful and nothing to be ashamed of. Theo had only positive sexual experiences until he met me." The familiar wave of shame enveloped me. "I don't know why he stayed with me so long."

"He's still with you. He loves you. I could see it in his eyes and feel it in the air when he visited."

"Thank you," I told her.

I didn't know exactly what was happening, but I could feel the pain and trauma of my childhood leaving my body. The hurt reminded me of when I had a staph infection. I submerged my leg in a hot bath and all this gross, but kind of cool looking stuff would drain out. It stung like crazy, but I could tell it was a healing sting. The same thing was happening to my heart. It hurt, but I was finally beginning to heal.

Chapter Twenty-One

ONE SUNDAY

"MORNIN' MA'AM! BEAUTIFUL SUNRISE, ISN'T IT?" THE JOGGER said, passing me by as I meandered along the lakefront. The wind was whipping my red dress against my body, and I grasped the hem with both hands to avoid flashing him my underwear.

I must have looked out of place that morning with my day-old makeup and low cut, cleavage-baring dress and heels. I was on my way home from a night of dancing, a night I didn't want to end. I had never danced much in the past, but I was becoming more comfortable in my skin and learning to move to the music in ways that I still considered a little scandalous.

After living in NOLA for almost four months, the city was starting to feel like home. I had been to six festivals and interviewed dozens of people about their experiences with and since Hurricane Katrina, Keira had introduced me to the best local shops, and I was beginning to get a true sense of what it meant to be on New Orleans time.

I had recently started venturing out of the city, spending many Sunday mornings jogging along Lake Pontchartrain. New Orleanians love to cook and they love to eat. It's the only place I've ever been where people discuss where they're going to eat next time they go out to dinner, while they're out eating dinner. Since so much of life in New Orleans revolved around food, it became necessary to find time to exercise, so I began driving my little Honda Civic to Lakeshore Drive and jogging along the lake. On this one Sunday morning, however, I wasn't looking to burn off calories; I was there to soak up the sunrise and have some quiet time with myself.

While I didn't miss the institution of church, I did miss the community I sometimes found there and that feeling of connection to the divine. I sat down on the grass, staring into the water. The lake stretches out over 20 miles, so as I gazed over the water it seemed like I was looking out into the ocean; nothing but water as far as I could see. I inhaled deeply and deliberately, bringing myself fully into the moment. Slowly, I exhaled, trying to free my body of its familiar inner turmoil.

Breathe in ... Breathe out.

Breathe in ... Breathe out.

The lake was my church. There were no offerings, no trendy rock band, no coffee shops or bookstores, no megaphones or video screens. No sin, no shame, no judgement. Just pure, unadulterated love and appreciation. The peace I felt on those Sunday mornings by the water far exceeded "the peace of God that passes all understanding" I was promised in church.

Divinity was all around me. It wasn't tied to my knowledge about the Bible, it wasn't dependent upon my actions, seen or unseen. These waters were tranquil and the air, reverent. I knew then that God was with me. God moved through me. God loved me. God was love and love was God. God was more than Christianity; Christianity was not God.

I wanted to call my Christian friend Beth to tell her what I was thinking. Beth was a good Christian, as opposed to me, a bad one. Our mutual love of writing had brought us together--that and the fact that, while Beth herself was heavily involved in church, she didn't care much about what anyone else did. She was blissfully unaware of how much pain the church caused me. This was partly because I hid it, but also because she chose not to see it.

I wanted someone who was a Christian to acknowledge that what I felt was divine, even though I knew that wasn't possible. Such is the nature of the unseen world that surrounds us; it requires trust in things unproven. But interestingly, while I knew my experience with the divine outside of the church would be dismissed, I remembered how unquestioningly they had believed me when I told them I had encountered divinity in the form of Christianity. They accepted my experiences and thoughts as a result of divine intervention, viewing my life as confirmation of their own beliefs and hopes.

Of course, even though I'm obviously the same person whose account of how God moved in my life was completely valid in their minds, I knew they wouldn't believe my experience with divinity at the lakefront. The thought angered me. I didn't need their validation, but I craved it.

I started thinking about how my mom wasn't able to show her true self at church. At home, she was strong willed-- submissive to my dad, but strong willed in general. She also worked outside the home during a time when it was uncommon for mothers to do so, but she didn't mention that to the other church ladies. Instead, she squeezed in Bible studies when her swing shift schedule lined up with the weekday morning time slot. She also smoked cigarettes, a habit she developed before she became a Christian, but one she couldn't quite kick no matter how hard she prayed.

Growing up, I resented her for smoking. Christians weren't supposed to smoke. In my righteous indignation, I thought of her as a hypocrite; a phony. I judged my mom for behaving one way at home and another at church.

That day at the lake with the wind in my hair and the sun beating on my back, I finally saw the truth: my mom wasn't *allowed* to be herself at church. She had to conform to their standards, or she would not have been accepted.

Part of me wonders if the self-proclaimed Christians I know are the ones who are lost. When I was immersed in evangelicalism, I was more confused than I am now. While I have some amazing Christian friends, they seem to be the exception. For the most part, when I look at Christians I see self-righteous people who need to keep putting others down so they can feel spiritually superior. They were told they were "set apart by God" and "not of this world", but in many cases, they behave worse than the "worldly" folks they condemn. My atheist friends don't judge people for making choices about their own lives. I'm not Wiccan, but I love their mantra: "If it harms none, do as you will." Such a simple philosophy, in the same family as Jesus's command to, "Love your neighbor as yourself."

I had so many questions growing up, but whenever they got too deep, my mom's answers were always some version of, "God's ways are not our ways, honey". These deflected questions usually revolved around God and how to ensure I didn't go to hell. I was told that Jesus dying on the cross for our sins would get me into heaven. My mom said it was true, my grandma said it was true, my church, where my uncle was the pastor, said it was true, so I believed it: Jesus died for me. I answered dozens of altar calls when I was growing up, but it never seemed to take. I still didn't feel "saved".

Fear is present in my earliest memories of my life: fear of dying, fear of going to hell; even fear of going to heaven, because my mom had told me she wouldn't be my mom in heaven. As a child, I thought it meant I would be alone. To fear both heaven and hell meant that I feared death to the point of dread.

I looked out at the lake that surrounded me. Fear had kept its grip on me for far too long. I wanted to be free, once and for all. As I surveyed the waters before me, I became aware that I could fall in, hit my head on a rock, and be gone from this life in an instant.

I stood up barefoot, holding my heels in one hand, and moved toward the edge of the lake, maneuvering down onto the rocks in the water.

"I wonder if it would hurt." I thought, contemplating death with a newfound sense of freedom.

The winds were picking up and the waves crashed onto the rocks beneath my feet, splashing my ankles.

I am in control. I have the power of life and death in my hands. I could choose to leap off these rocks, never to be heard from again.

I leaned into the feeling. Fear caused my entire body to tremble, begging me to step back onto the grass.

Instead I stayed, inching closer to death. I wanted to overcome this crippling fear that had kept me from loving and from living.

I closed my eyes, lifted my face toward the sky, and expressed my gratitude to the universe. I turned my attention to the cosmos; the great energy that connects all creatures, big and small, to one another and to nature. A newfound appreciation swelled in my heart. Gratitude enveloped me. I was grateful for my life, my parents, my friends. I was grateful for Theo's unconditional love and unwavering support. I was grateful for Keira and our unique relationship. I was grateful for the city of New Orleans and the wonderful people I had met during my interviews.

When I was done giving thanks, I turned toward the shore, climbed the concrete steps, and sat back down on the grass for a few minutes. Feeling light and at peace, I got into my car and drove home.

Chapter Twenty-Two

NO REGRETS

IF I HAD ONLY...I SHOULD'VE...WHY DIDN'T I...

Regret comes in many forms: wishing we had done something instead of nothing, doing something we wish we hadn't, and most commonly, not doing something we wish we had.

I used to carry around so many regrets. I would second-guess every decision and beat myself up about every choice I made, no matter how insignificant. I regretted going so far with Jacob when we were dating and shortly after our breakup, but once I started to heal from my sexual shame, I regretted not going further with him. To me, Jacob was like dessert for someone raised on a sugar-free diet. Sugar was all around, but I wasn't allowed to eat it. Birthday cakes, cookies, candy, ice cream: all off-limits. I could see it; I could smell it; but I could never have that cupcake.

Then the cupcake got divorced, and I found myself on a marriage vacation and in the same city as the cupcake.

I wanted to satisfy my craving, but Jacob and I weren't even speaking. Things had gone awry the weekend we evacuated. Old hurts bubbled to the surface, and he was on the receiving end of my "healing". It hurt to find out he had lied about me. I had compassion for him as well, given the immense pressure he was under. He was a good guy. He had a kind heart. I wanted to judge him for what he did, but the pressures we were under in our faith community caused all of us to act out of character. Still, while I wanted to talk to him, I really didn't know how to reach out.

I missed Jacob. I wanted him. It took every ounce of my willpower to stop myself from texting him. I went to his Instagram and scrolled through pictures of him and his friends, a couple of group photos that included his ex-wife, some of his border collie and all his stunning New Orleans landscape photos. During my social media stalking (because what else can you call it), I found a group picture from freshman year of college when Jacob and I were still together.

My mind went back to that night. It was an unusually cool April evening. We had just finished dinner when we handed our film camera to the server and asked her to snap this photo. We look like a happy couple, but the truth is our relationship was on shaky ground. The only reason I appear joyful is because earlier that day I had found out I would be spending the next semester abroad.

It's a good thing Jacob and I broke up mere days after that photo was taken, because I met Theo the next semester.

"So, you're in Texas as a foreign exchange student from Berlin, and you're doing a semester abroad in London?" I asked, speaking my first words to the man I would marry.

We met the night of the Study Abroad introductory meet and greet. The administration explained all the standard rules and expectations for students as they offered a chance for us to meet the people we'd be spending a lot of time with in the coming weeks.

"No, I think it's clever. I would've never thought to do that." He charmed me instantly, with his understated personality. Theo wasn't wildly popular among groups of people, but he was, without a doubt, the one everybody enjoyed talking to most.

"I love to travel," Theo confessed. "And even though I've only been back in the states a few months, I am ready to take a vacation. This way, I don't miss out on my education, and I get to meet great people from outside my major." He looked at me as if to imply I was "great people". I found it difficult not to swoon.

Theo and I became fast friends. I was in awe of his comfortable confidence. He wasn't arrogant like most guys who looked as good as he did. He had a quiet self-assurance that attracted me to him. He could easily draw me in with his deep, honey colored eyes. It has been said that the eyes are the window to the soul, and Theo's soul was beautiful.

"What do you think this life is for?" He asked me one evening as we sat on the rooftop balcony of our student housing complex.

"If you had asked me a few months ago, I would've given you a completely different answer, but right now, all I can tell you is I have no idea."

"Me neither, but I'm trying to live it to the fullest." Theo spoke with an accent, but not a very thick one. He explained that he was born in Germany to a German dad and American mom. They met at a marketing conference in London. I couldn't help but let my mind wander. *Would we have a similar story to tell? Would I have a husband from Germany?* I knew we had just met, and I was only a few months out of my relationship with Jacob, but what was developing between Theo and me was happening effortlessly.

I was attracted to him, but I stayed focused on my studies. I even picked up a couple of freelance writing gigs while abroad, which gave me the chance to type using the English spelling for words like *colour, paediatric* and *neigbour*. For no explicable reason, it made me giddy.

Theo was respectfully persistent in his pursuit of a connection with me. He didn't seem like he was trying to date me, instead, he seemed to truly wanted to get to know me. We spent hours walking around the city. One night we were meeting some classmates for dinner at a restaurant along the River Thames. Theo suggested I bring a coat, but I was sure I wouldn't be cold. After dinner, we walked along the river and I realized what a mistake it was to leave my coat at home. Theo gave me a knowing look, and I averted my eyes to hide my embarrassment. Instead of shaming me, he opened his arms so I could position myself inside his jacket. The warmth from his body sent a shiver down my spine. While I believe love grows slowly over time, my feelings for him leveled up big time on that crisp fall night in London.

Looking back on our life and our story, I realized that no matter where this journey takes us, I can say without a doubt that when it comes to falling in love with Theo, I have no regrets.

Chapter Twenty-Three

KATRINA STORY

"I hate the smell of citronella," Ann, my interviewee, told me as she clicked her lighter and lit the pungent candle. "But the heat just won't quit, so the mosquitoes won't die off." I wasn't sure if she realized that's evidence of climate change, but she sure wasn't happy about having to breathe the burned citrus scent while we sat at her picnic table and chatted over a glass of iced tea.

"So, what do you want to know?" she asked me, cutting straight to the point.

"I'd love to hear your Katrina story, and I'm interested in how it has shaped your feelings about New Orleans, particularly during hurricane season." I replied.

Ann seemed a little harsh, but she was refreshingly honest and up-front about who she was. She had no interest in trying to impress me. She squeezed three lemon wedges into her mason jar of sweet tea and recounted her story.

"It was the Friday before the storm, and the workday was almost over. All I wanted to do was relax over the weekend.

On my way out of the office, I told my colleagues to have a good weekend and that I'd see them Monday. Little did I know, it was my last day at the office. It wasn't until the evening of Friday, August 26th that I even knew there was a storm. I called a friend, because people called each other back then, to see what her weekend plans were. When she told me she was keeping an eye on the hurricane, I couldn't hide my shock. She went on to explain that Hurricane Katrina, which was supposed to only be an issue for central Florida, had looped around and was back in the Gulf.

Until that year, evacuating for me was nothing more than a forced vacation. We'd go out of town for a few days and come back to normal life every other year or so. I figured it would be the same thing for Katrina. We packed up a few clothes and headed north Saturday morning. I figured we would be back to the grind by Wednesday, Thursday at the latest. When we left for Dallas around 8:00am on Saturday, no one was too concerned about this storm. By evening, people began to change their minds.

In the early hours of the morning on Sunday, August 28th, Katrina became a Category 4 heading straight for New Orleans. Thousands upon thousands of people took to the roads, fleeing the city in all directions, sitting in traffic for up to 20 hours to get to safety. That's when we realized this was nothing like previous storms.

You know the rest. The levees broke, the waters rose, people couldn't get home, those at home couldn't get out. Thousands died. Countless more lost everything they owned. Tragedy befell our city. The news coverage left me broken. We failed those who needed us most. The ones without the means to protect themselves. My husband and I were lucky.

Our house didn't get a lot of damage, and most of our belongings remained intact. However, we were stranded in a new city where we hardly knew anyone.

We agonized over whether we should stay in Dallas or go back to New Orleans time and again before we ultimately decided to start our lives in Dallas. We got jobs. We rented an apartment. We made new friends. It was easier than I expected, yet harder at the same time. I spent several nights crying, wondering if we made the right decision. Ultimately, I believe it was. It strengthened my marriage, boosted my confidence, and brought me closer to my family in Texas. But our story didn't end there.

A little over a year after our unexpected move, I came back to New Orleans for business. In the week I was here, I fell more in love with New Orleans than ever. Growing up here had left me indifferent to the amazing things this city has to offer. I took our unique culture for granted. But there was something about post-Katrina New Orleans that made me realize all I had missed about our city, and that week I knew we had to come home. We were happy in Dallas. We had created a nice little life for ourselves and were surrounded by great people, but it wasn't home. When I returned, I was curious how my husband would respond to my change of heart. Surprisingly, he had been thinking about moving back as well! Within two months, we were back where we belong, and more proud than ever to call New Orleans home."

"How do you feel about the New Orleans you returned to?" I asked Ann.

"I don't know how much of it is the 'new' New Orleans, and how much of it is my perspective, but as the years go on, I fall more in love with this city. I love how everyone knows someone that you know. I love the shops on Magazine Street, the Frenchmen Art Market and all the new restaurants. I love that New Orleans is truly a city that lives in you. Like most locals, there are still some things I would change about New Orleans, but I am happy to say that we are planting roots here. I have learned to never say never, but I have no plans to leave again. New Orleans is a place I am proud to call home."

Her story wasn't spectacular, but it was moving. Ann suffered little loss, but even so, Katrina fundamentally changed her and her view of New Orleans. I started to wonder how I would feel about my home once I returned. In a way that is nothing like her story at all, I could understand why she fell in love with the new New Orleans. It had been surprisingly easy for me to adapt to the city's culture. I made new friends and I hadn't missed a beat with work, turning in content for various websites week after week plus working on my Katrina story. Yet I was well aware that my stay was temporary, and I'd soon go home to Texas the way Ann returned to New Orleans. While Austin may not have changed in my absence, how much would my life?

"And how are your hurricane seasons now?" I asked her.

"Well, the first few years were fine. I felt like, okay, we endured this major, life altering and infrastructure changing event, now we get a break. But with each passing year, I feel a growing sense of dread that our number will be pulled again, and if that happens, will our resilience prevail? I really don't know if we can survive another great loss. I want to say we are capable and prepared, but deep in my heart, I don't think we are. I'm almost... Waiting for the other shoe to drop." She said, just before asking if I wanted to switch out my tea for a cocktail.

I wanted to keep talking, but I could tell that was the end of our interview.

Her story felt bigger than it sounded on its face. I didn't know why, I just related to Ann's experience. It wasn't anywhere near as tragic as most everyone else I spoke to, but it made an impact on me. Maybe it was the fact that her suffering wasn't great, but it was life-altering nonetheless. She reminded me of me in a way I couldn't put my finger on. I was inspired by how comfortable she was in her own skin, how matter-of-fact she was with her story, and her take-no-bullshit attitude.

I wondered if she was right. Was New Orleans on shaky ground? Could another storm decimate it beyond repair? From what I saw of the people of New Orleans, it would take a lot more than another Katrina to slow down their tenacity.

Gathering these stories of people from all walks of life was gut wrenching, uplifting, heartbreaking, and inspiring. They humbled me. Everyone has a story to tell, and in New Orleans, almost everyone had a Katrina story worth sharing.

Chapter Twenty-Four

HALLOWEEN NIGHT

"OH, EXCUSE ME." I HEARD A FAMILIAR VOICE SAY AS WE strolled down Frenchmen Street.

For Halloween, Keira and I dressed as sexy versions of Little Red Riding Hood and The Big Bad Wolf. I wore a grey corset top with a plaid schoolgirl type skirt and fuzzy grey boots, topping my look off with a grey pointy-eared headband. Keira's Little Red Riding Hood costume consisted of a red robe draped over a white ribbed tank top and little red shorts; she completed her look with a pair of red Converse because Keira didn't like high heels.

I lost my Halloween virginity in New Orleans. Until that point, my experience with Halloween was limited to my church's Hallelujah Night, which was just like its secular counterpart, complete with costumes and candy, but because we claimed it was for Jesus, it was less taboo than getting together with our neighbors.

I was conditioned to be afraid of Halloween, also known by Evangelicals as the "Devil's Holiday". When I was about six years old, someone got hit by a car around the corner from my church during Hallelujah Night, and I remember saying, "*and on Halloween*" in an ominous tone, as though the night itself brought on the accident. I had long since gotten over my fears, or so I had thought. Maybe the reason I always opted to stay home and give out candy was because I didn't want to risk anything happening to me on what I used to know as the scariest day of the year. It was time to see what Halloween was truly all about, and what better place than New Orleans to do it?

Our night on Frenchmen Street was one I'll never forget. Whistles and lustful stares came from all directions. We were not just hot, but "people think it's okay to stare at you like you're not a human" hot. Exhilaration and a tinge of fear flowed through my veins. I was the Big Bad Wolf, and I was out to devour someone on the Devil's holiday. Men started to look like prey; I met their primal "I want you" stares with my own, only stronger. So strong, a few of them cowered down and looked away. Of course. Weak men can't stand strong women.

Either he bumped into her or she bumped into him, I'm not sure, but once I heard the voice behind me, I turned my head to see Jacob apologizing to Keira. My heart stopped.

"Oh my god hiiiiii!" I said. My tone always goes peak white girl in awkward situations.

"Keira, this is Jacob." My mouth formed the words, but what my face communicated to her was "This is *the* Jacob. The one I've been yammering on and on about *ad nauseam*."

Thus far, I had done a pretty decent job compartmentalizing my life. If I was going to be free to act however I wanted, I couldn't have the girl I'm in a "friends with benefits" situation with meet the guy I broke up with so I could remain pure! Yet here I was.

After a few uncomfortable minutes of talking in the crowded street, the five of us; Keira and me plus Jacob and two of his friends, decided to head into a bar where an 80's throwback band was about to take the stage. We found a booth along the wall and Jacob ordered us a round of drinks.

As the evening progressed, any sense of awkwardness that had been between Jacob and me began melting away. We fell right back into our groove. He updated me on his life, including the fact that he was casually dating someone. I told him how my article was coming along and the crazy story about how I got my Honda Civic, strategically leaving out the more intimate details about Sean. I learned that night just how much things had shifted between us. We were never going to be as close as we had been, and though I wanted him desperately, it seemed more apparent than ever that the feeling wasn't mutual.

It wasn't until the chorus began that I realized what song was playing.

"Oh my gosh let's go dance!" Keira grabbed my hand and led me to the makeshift dance floor in the middle of the bar as Pour Some Sugar on me belted through the speakers.

Keira and I joined the chorus, singing and twisting our bodies as though we were auditioning for a burlesque show.

As more and more girls crowded the dance floor, the energy in the room turned from playful to sultry.

Leaning into the public display of affection Keira and I had going, the world around me stopped. I became the main character in the story, and all that mattered was me. My needs. My desires. My pleasure. I did what I wanted without regard for anything or anyone else. We danced closely. Too close. When the music stopped, I looked around and Jacob was gone.

Did I ruin things between us? Did he know now that I was bisexual? Keira and I were pretty comfortable together. Too comfortable. Like, we've-seen-each-other-naked comfortable. I lay in bed replaying the events of the evening.

The "Great to see you, let's make plans to catch up soon" text he sent me the next morning didn't offer me much insight. Was it really great to see me? When did he want to catch up? How soon is 'soon'? Did my overtly sexy dance with Keira freak him out? Turn him on? All these questions burned in my mind as I replied, "You too. And definitely!" We never did make plans to catch up.

Chapter Twenty-Five

CHILDHOOD DREAMS

"MY FIRST CHILDHOOD DREAM WAS TO BE A WRITER. WELL, MY second, actually. My first was to be a grocery store clerk, but that's neither here nor there." I sat down with Jill, recounting my childhood. Weekly therapy was my sanity during my stay in New Orleans.

I told Jill about a story I wrote when I was eight, starring me and my best friend. It was a made-up adventure that was far more exciting than my mundane life, but the feelings in the story were true. In my mind, it was a great way to get out my complex, growing feelings for people outside my immediate family. Around the time I had my first best friend, which was 3rd grade, I also had my first crush. It was on a boy named Ryan who gave me a cartoon Valentine's Day card that read, "Shhhh, it's a secret, I like you," and on the other side he penned a note about how much he loved me. I made up a love story about Ryan and me, and promptly tore it up so my parents wouldn't find it.

Telling stories, telling truth inside of fiction, felt natural to me. Expressing myself through the words on the page, even if the stories weren't real, was a safe way for me to communicate my feelings. As a child, I thought I would grow up to be an author.

Somewhere between children's church and youth group, my childhood dreams turned from being a writer to being a wife and mom. Don't get me wrong, I can't remember a time when I didn't want those things, but they were not my first dream. I had dreams of being more than a person whose identity is wrapped up in who she is to other people."

"What do you think brought on the change?" Jill asked.

"I don't know," I sighed. I described how, when I was around 9 or 10 years old, the church separated the children's church by gender for services. I didn't think much about being separated from the boys at the time, though I realize now that's when they revved up the purity culture teachings. Being someone who wanted to do well and please others, I bought into this teaching hook, line, and sinker. Even when I spent a year and a half not going to church, I still dressed the part of a "good Christian". I didn't date or do anything wrong. Even that turned out to be a trap, because I could feel myself getting prideful and judgmental. Why couldn't anyone else just follow the rules? They were laid out clear as day. Step by step, you could be a good Christian. I started to hate who I had become. They taught us to worship at the altar of marriage and motherhood. The virgin who marries and brings forth children is approved by God. To be anything else was to be inferior at best, ostracized at worst.

"Gosh, Hillary, this stuff is so heavy. Sometimes, when you open up like this, your pain fills the air." Jill told me gently, causing me to break down sobbing.

The salt of my tears heaped relief upon my broken heart. I let out a guttural moan that would've had the men from the gospels thinking I was demon-possessed.

"Well, I guess this is an exorcism then," I said, breaking into a moment of laughter.

"Look, your pain, it's leaving you. It's not a demon. It's shame and self-loathing. It's the regret of a life not lived. You are entitled to those feelings. Making space for them to move through you the way you just did allows them to leave your body. You are hurting, but you are also healing."

I couldn't believe how damaged I had been. I spent so much of my life convincing myself that I was fine, things weren't *that* bad, and maybe comparatively speaking, they weren't. I know in the grand scheme of things, my problems were of the "first world" variety: I grew up a straight, white, middle-class, Christian woman. I couldn't deny my privilege. Nonetheless, the experience of human suffering, though varied in degrees, is universal. When we opened the Pandora's Box that was my identity, I was shocked at how much bullshit I had to work through.

Jill encouraged me to write my feelings, whatever came to mind about my past. I created a poem one morning, my fingers flying across the keyboard as the words poured out of me faster than I could type. I almost didn't know what I was feeling until the words flowed out of my fingertips:

> **It's not what they told me. It's what they showed me.**

> *They told me that I was saved by grace. They showed me that works earned favor.*

They told me to be a good Samaritan. They showed me how to cross the road.

They told me to be sexually pure. They showed me they could get away with anything.

They told me to welcome the least of these. They showed me disdain for the poor.

They told me 'love one another'. They showed me how to love ones that fit the mold.

They told me to be humble. They showed me how to live extravagantly.

They told me to live above reproach. They showed me hypocrisy.

They told me God so loved the world. They showed me disdain for the other.

They told me to forgive. They showed me judgement.

They told me to trust. They showed me lies.

They told me to make peace. They showed me how to be an enemy.

They told me we were sinners, worthy of death. They showed me they think they are better than the rest.

A sacred silence enveloped the room. Finally, my pain was named, in the safety of Jill's office where it was acknowledged in a way it deserved.

"Your pain is real," she told me, knowing I needed validation more than anything.

Just like at the lakefront, I left therapy feeling a little bit lighter. Another emotional weight had been lifted.

I spent the next week in Baton Rouge, where I had the opportunity to interview officials at the state capitol about the government's response to the aftermath of Hurricane Katrina. Aside from my scheduled interviews, I had decided to keep to myself for 6 whole days: No texting, no calling. No hookups, no friends, no therapy. I was going to take some time to enjoy life. I read an entire novel called Memoirs of a Geisha, which is a fictional memoir that reads like a true story and is filled with genuine emotion, but is very much a made-up story (*wink*).

Self-care was my primary goal for the week; I needed a break from the wild vacation life I had been living these last five months. Even though caring for myself was the theme of my time in New Orleans, I had quickly gotten swept up in friendships and relationships, and I now needed time to process everything. This week off from everything, both my real life and my New Orleans life, was exactly what I needed. I visited a college bar and heard a local band play; I took an introductory Kickboxing class at a gym; I even had my nails and toes manicured, which was something I hadn't done in years. I walked around the gorgeous Louisiana State University campus, watched trashy reality TV, and took baths with bath bombs and candles. One of the days, I only left my hotel bed to meet my interviewee.

Baton Rouge was only about an hour from New Orleans, but the culture was completely different. Thankfully, the southern charm remained. I enjoyed small talk with strangers in line at coffee shops so I didn't get too lonely.

On the 1.5-hour drive back, panic set in. I would soon be

wrapping up my time in New Orleans and heading to an uncertain future. Would my marriage survive? What about these lingering feelings for Jacob? Would Keira and I stay friends? How would Theo react to knowing what (and whom) I've done? Instead of contemplating these big questions, I turned on my "girl power" playlist and jammed out to Pink, Stevie Nicks, Paramore, and Madonna all the way home. I allowed the music to be a form of self-care, or at least, a good avoidance tactic. I knew I had a lot to deal with, but for the time being, I was content to belt out the lyrics to Landslide, using my pen as a microphone and looking like a complete idiot to anyone who happened to pass me by on the interstate.

Everything about who I was and thought I'd be was being destroyed in a landslide of my own making, and I wasn't the least bit sorry.

Chapter Twenty-Six

BREWING STORM

"DON'T FORGET, WE HAVE A SHOWING THIS WEEKEND!" MY realtor texted me a reminder about yet another open house.

The lease on my shotgun double was almost up, which meant I had to devote a lot more time to cleaning my place, as potential occupants traipsed through my living quarters on a regular basis. I had never realized how protective I was of my personal space until I had to watch as people stomped through it, critiquing my art choices as if they had anything to do with the house. I'm sorry you preferred "something from Kirkland's" instead of original work from local artists, Linda.

Since hurricane season was coming to an end, I began packing away the life I built in New Orleans. As I began boxing up my many newly acquired belongings (thanks to the ubiquitous nature of local street art in this city), I started the process of letting go of the relationships I had built with people there. I slowly stopped frequenting my favorite local coffee shop, the one where I met Angelique, who led me not only to my car, which was now for sale, but to Sean, who turned out to be a friend, lead character in my fantasies, amazing lover, and one of the main narratives in my piece on Hurricane Katrina. I wasn't doing this entirely out of deliberation, rather, my work was winding down. I was poring over all the stories I had gathered, and since I cursed a lot more during this part of the process, I decided it best I work from my kitchen table where no one heard my profanity-laden plea for this piece to just fucking come together already.

I also distanced myself from Keira toward the end of my stay. I knew how much I would miss her, so I decided to start getting used to her not being part of my everyday life. She was busy with her story anyway, so it wasn't too hard. I met her and her mom friends a few times for playdates, but not much else. She'd met a guy on Halloween night and started dating him shortly thereafter, so it was the perfect time to loosen our bond.

My last Sunday in New Orleans, I was downtown visiting a museum featuring a Living Katrina exhibit. I had bought all the books I could find and read all the news stories, from national television to local papers to independent bloggers and people I met at the pharmacy, but this was my first time experiencing an interactive exhibit documenting Katrina and the Southeast's recovery. All of the stories I'd collected were brought to life as I came face to face with items like a coast guard rescue basket used to rescue people off the rooftops of their flooded homes, a recreated attic with a hole chopped in the roof, and a garage door with search and rescue markings. Knowing I had passed those very same search and rescue markings on houses in the city, the magnitude of Katrina's impact, and how much more rebuilding the city still needed weighed heavily on me. I let out a silent prayer, "God, if you're there, please let my article be a small part in helping rebuild New Orleans."

After the museum's exhibit ripped a hole in my heart and caused me to ache for the loss Katrina brought to this rich, beautiful city, I needed a day drink. I popped into a quintessential New Orleans dive bar and ordered myself a Bloody Mary in a to-go cup. I wandered around the French Quarter, and ended up in Louis Armstrong Park. I had been there before for one of the summer festivals, and today was no different. Music was playing and people were eating, drinking, and dancing, but the vendor booths with local makers selling arts and crafts were noticeably smaller at this fest. As I got closer to the main stage, I felt the music calling me. The heavy, intricate bass lines pulled me in closer. Everyone near the stage was dancing, no bystanders to be seen. Without thinking twice, I joined the revelers. I don't really know how to dance, but that day, my body did. I felt myself moving almost involuntarily. No one was paying attention to me, and if they were, their opinion didn't matter anyway. Once again, I was the main character in my story. It wasn't until the sun started to go down that I realized how long I had been there moving to the music, letting go of all my thoughts, fears, and concerns. There were no breaks in the music to indicate it was time to stop dancing. I was lost in the rhythm, seemingly absent from my body yet more present in it than ever. My experience on the makeshift dance floor at Louis Armstrong Park was just as spiritual an experience as my day at the lakefront. I was finding God, holiness, and purity in nature and in art. I stayed until the winds began to pick up and the last of the sunlight was eclipsed by thick, dark clouds, before racing home to try to beat the brewing storm.

I had just finished showering, my hair still damp, and I was wearing only a bathrobe when I heard a knock at my door. I attempted to throw clothes on, but the knocking became more vigorous, so I grabbed my cell phone and a broom stick, in case it was a serial killer.

I looked through the paned glass on the side of the door and saw Jacob standing there stone-faced, his clothes soaked from the torrential rain.

"What is THIS?" he asked indignantly, holding up his cell phone.

"I... I don't know. What is it?" Water droplets were covering the phone's screen, obscuring my view of whatever it was that Jacob was finding so offensive.

He slammed one hand onto the porch railing and held out his phone with the other.

"It's your dating profile." His expression was a combination of confusion, anger, and hurt.

I felt like a deer in headlights. I didn't know what to say or how to respond. A kid with their hand in the cookie jar. A dog caught with its owner's favorite shoe in his mouth. I was busted. I hadn't wanted Jacob to find out anything about the real reason I was here, and I certainly hadn't wanted him to find out like this. I said the first thing that popped into my mind.

"I thought you weren't on dating apps?!" I exclaimed stupidly.

"I wasn't. But I am now." He shot back. "Why are *you* on them?!" he demanded.

I wanted to be honest with him, but I couldn't find my words. I wanted him to know how badly I wanted him, how hard it was to keep my composure while I was in his presence.

"I... It's... It's a really long story. Do you want to come inside, out of this weather?" I asked. The wind picked up and started blowing leaves and raindrops onto my porch.

"No." He started to walk away. I didn't want to let him, but what could I say? I stood there, frozen, feeling the weight of my silence.

When he got to his car, he turned back. Ignoring the fact that he was being drenched, he yelled, "I want to know why! Why, if you are available, why wouldn't you want to be with me?"

Nothing else needed to be said. I ran to him, almost tripping down the porch steps. I threw my arms around him and kissed him hungrily. Everything stilled around us as the rain soaked through our clothes. Jacob: the present I could never open, the rare artifact I wished to admire; the cupcake I wanted to devour.

We moved in unison to the porch, our bodies never losing contact, lips locked together with the tension that had been building between us all these months. The urgency of years of desire pushed us into the house. I both wanted to devour him in one bite and savor every inch of him little by little.

It was happening after all this time. Jacob, my first love and first heartbreak, was in my house, kissing my practically naked body.

I can still feel his lips on the side of my neck. My hands gripping the sheets. His body on mine, mine on his. A moment 10 years in the making and we didn't want to miss a thing. No curve was untouched, no freckle unseen. We spent hours in foreplay. And when we finally came together, it was everything I hoped it would be and more. I was so overcome with emotion I shed a tear, and... were those... fireworks?

"You did hear fireworks," Jacob informed me, as I was gushing over how great the sex had been. "The Saints are playing tonight; they probably just scored a touchdown."

As the post-orgasm high wore off, we looked at each other and we both knew we had reached the end of our journey. Everything that had built up between Jacob and me had culminated into one unforgettable night.

The understanding between us was unspoken; nothing more needed to be said. We talked instead about my upcoming move, promised to stay friends, and that was that.

While I felt a twinge of sadness knowing it was over, I was mostly relieved. There were no more lingering "what-ifs" about Jacob. We had finally finished something we'd begun years before, something we were able to experience because of our wonder for what might have been.

Chapter Twenty-Seven

ABOUT SEX

"I CAN'T BELIEVE YOU'RE GOING HOME IN LESS THAN A WEEK," Keira's text message read. It was followed by several crying-face emojis.

"I know," I replied. I didn't have enough emojis to convey how I was feeling. Excited. Terrified. Anxious. Sad. Hopeful.

This trip changed me. The work I had done on myself, which began years ago, had prepared the soil. In New Orleans, where you don't have to go far to find a celebration, where everyone is your neighbor, in the city where you can leave your pretense at the door and, rather than hide your crazy, parade it down the street, I blossomed into the woman I was always meant to be.

"See you tonight?" Keira wrote back.

"Can't wait," I said. It was true; I couldn't wait to be with Keira again. I wanted to laugh with her and cry with her and connect with her. I loved her body. I loved how good she could make me feel. But more than that, I needed her presence. Her quiet confidence. My eyes burned with unshed tears when I thought about it being our last night together.

When Keira arrived at my now-barren shotgun double, she looked like she had been crying. We hugged, cried, and cried some more. Then we wiped our tears, picked up take-out from our favorite deli, and cracked open a couple of beers. Keira made me laugh all the time. She made me feel good. Special. Accepted. She had her own issues like navigating life as a single mom and exploring her sexuality for the first time, but she didn't have the added shame of purity culture.

Keira had become, without a doubt, my best friend. She knew things about me that no one else did. Because I was able to be open with her about my life and marriage, I opened up to her about everything else. She had seen both me and my husband naked. She knew all about my upbringing. We shared a love of people and of writing. What would become of this relationship when I returned to Austin?

"It's too bad you can't move to Austin. They have good public schools there." I jokingly said, trying to entice her with schools because the school system in New Orleans needed so much work.

"Ha, as if Brad would let that fly." She giggled.

"It's too bad you can't just stay here," she suggested, running her hand across the same flowery sheets that had adorned the mattress when I first arrived six months earlier, motioning for me to join her on the bed.

"In a perfect world, you could be my sister-wife," I laughed as I stripped off my clothes and crawled up the bed toward her.

Before coming to New Orleans, I had been ashamed of my nakedness in more ways than one. The combination of purity culture messaging and mainstream pop culture had me believing that my body existed for men and yet was harmful to men, while also not being attractive enough for men. I didn't want anyone to see me naked. I didn't even want to see myself naked.

Thanks to my time in New Orleans, I could stand naked and unashamed in front of men or women but, most importantly, I could stand naked in front of a mirror.

Being naked with Keira wasn't always about sex. We often spent time together naked, or at most, in a thin bathrobe. I didn't think much about it until I saw our naked bodies atop the floral sheets, but there had been a lot of nakedness in our friendship. Not just physical nakedness, either. We shared our deepest, darkest secrets with one another, along with our hopes and dreams and our biggest fears. Our connection was similar in a way to my connection with Theo. We didn't have the history or the exclusive nature of a couple relationship, but she was my strongest connection aside from him.

Keira kissed my mouth, then moved down to my neck. She made her way to my shoulders as she spoke softly.

She kissed my chest. "I."

She kissed my nipple. "Am."

She kissed my stomach. "Going to."

She kissed me lower. "Miss."

She pointed her bright pink fingernail at my appendix scar. "This."

"I'm going to miss all of you." I told her, pulling her back up toward me. Our last night together was heartwarming and sad and fun and steamy. Of all my experiences in New Orleans, I was most grateful to have met Keira. When we said our goodbyes the next day I was sad, but it didn't feel final the way it had with Jacob. Keira was going to be in my life. I promised to send her some of her favorite Ikea chocolate, and she and Quinn were planning to visit us in Austin over Mardi Gras. This wasn't the end of our story, just a transition.

Chapter Twenty-Eight

HOME AGAIN

"MY FLIGHT LANDS AT 11AM," I TEXTED THEO FOR THE FIRST time in months.

After what had felt simultaneously like a lifetime and the blink of an eye, I was on a plane headed back to Austin. The last time I saw Theo was the night he visited when we were with Keira. He replied with a simple, "K. See you when you get home."

My mind tried to analyze the text. Was he angry at me? Did he want a divorce? How much counseling would we need? I spent the time between the plane touching down and walking out of the airport trying to lull myself into a state of total acceptance. Whatever would be, would be. I gave this relationship my all; I did the work. I liberated myself from the purity culture I grew up in. I was still working through some of the hurts, but I'd made significant progress over the last six months. I was able to think about sex without feeling like I was doing something ungodly. I had done what I needed to do to heal, and the chips could fall where they may.

I stepped outside and took in my first breath of reality. Theo was standing across the aisle waiting for me. His eyes were full of longing as he rushed over and wrapped me into a giant hug, lifting me ever so slightly off the ground and telling me how much he had missed me. For the moment, all was right in the world. Just like before I left, we didn't want to let each other go, even to hop into the car that was waiting to take us home.

"We need to buy a car," I told him in an effort to cut the silence of the ride.

"But, parking is outrageous and we can both bike to work. Plus, with all these ride sharing apps, we can pretty much get anywhere at any time," he protested.

"You're right, it is easy to get along without a car here. It wasn't in New Orleans; I had to buy a car."

"How did you afford a car?" He asked.

"Funny you should ask!" I recounted the story about Angelique from the coffee shop and how she told me about the great deal on the Honda. For the time being, I decided it would be best to leave out the fact that I had sex with the seller of said Honda, and that he was now part of my article.

I was confused when our driver pulled up to a downtown hotel. "What are we doing here?"

"We aren't going home yet." Theo informed me with a twinkle in his eye. "I thought we could have a mini-vacation to decompress from our marriage vacation and reconnect... Perhaps in a hot tub?"

I let out a sigh of relief as things started to feel more relaxed with Theo. His planning a two-night stay at that hotel meant more to me than he could've imagined.

We opted not to talk about our physical encounters right away. Instead, we spent the next couple of days reconnecting physically, mentally, and emotionally.

We spent hours talking about my trip. I showed him some of the stories I had collected from Hurricane Katrina victims and we discussed my future plans. I told him how much I wanted to be an author. We talked about some ideas for books. A self-help book, a book about sex, or maybe even a story about my life, although I didn't and still don't feel like my life is interesting enough to garner a memoir.

"You are, without a doubt, my favorite person in the world," I told him, stroking his hair. "Some days, I missed you so much I wanted to drop everything and come home." I confessed.

"After I visited, I was ready to sell everything and meet you there." He told me.

"Ha! Our night was so good it made you want to move?" I chuckled.

Theo and I hardly got out of the bed when we were at the hotel except to get food and, of course, to visit the hot tub. On our second night there, after dinner and a couple of drinks, Theo brought up the night with Keira.

"I know we said we wouldn't discuss whatever physical encounters we had, but I can't help but wonder about Officer McHottie." He continued, "I'm curious how you knew her or if you... um... hired her?"

"Oh my gosh, no!!" I exclaimed. "Of course not." I am pro

sex-worker, but that was not something I had considered or explored.

I told Theo about Keira and how we had clicked immediately, and how awesome it was to have found a friend who was a writer. I told him how close we had become and that, if it wasn't awkward for him, she and her daughter wanted to visit when they had Mardi Gras.

"So, she's not actually a cop then, huh," Theo said with feigned disappointment. He always knew how to make me laugh.

"It sounds like she was a really important part of your time there," he said.

"She was. She is. I really hope she stays in my life, even if just as friends," I candidly confessed.

"Well, just so you know, the door to our marriage is always open if you're hooking up with chicks. Especially if I get to be a part of it," Theo announced.

That shameless, vulnerable confidence of Theo's used to make me feel small. It wasn't his fault; he was just so much more comfortable in his skin than I was in mine. Hearing his words, my immediate reaction was to recoil, but I realized I didn't have to recoil anymore.

"Thanks. I'll let you know." I giggled. At the time, I had no idea if I would be open to that. I loved being with Keira, but I didn't have a lingering desire to be with any other women. I started to wonder what that meant in terms of my sexuality. Was I bisexual? Or was Keira a unicorn?

Theo and I knew each other better than anyone else, but it became apparent during our first weekend back together that we were, in a way, meeting for the first time. I was no longer a submissive, timid, intimacy-challenged partner. I wasn't worried about religion anymore. For the first time, I was content with whatever relationship I had with the divine. I didn't need approval from Christianity. My time in New Orleans freed me from the chains of religion, and I was stronger and fiercer than ever, or so I thought.

Chapter Twenty-Nine

MY STORY

"DAMMIT! THIS ISN'T WORKING!" MY VOICE WAS GROWING louder as I became increasingly frustrated.

One afternoon shortly after I returned from my trip, Theo came home from work early to find me reeling. Rather than try to regain my composure, I let him witness my tantrum in all its glory.

"I thought everything would just flow. I thought it would be easy." I stood up from my desk, holding up a partially typed sheet of paper. "After all the time I spent in New Orleans, how can I have less than 1000 words in my story?? I have so much to write about, but the words just aren't coming!"

Theo calmly walked over and put his arms around me, kissing my forehead, making me feel safe. Once my breathing slowed, he gently reminded me who I was.

"You are an accomplished writer. You have written countless articles and journals. You have been featured in local and national publications. People pay you for your work. You can do this."

My husband's unwavering support has helped me over so many hurdles, this being no exception.

"I know that, but why is it so hard to believe?" I still faced self-doubt every time, with every assignment.

"Because you put a piece of your soul out there each time you publish something," he said. Theo had a gift for talking me off the ledge. It may have been a burden for him to bear, but he handled it with ease.

That day, my story began to take shape. The facts I had gathered, the stories I heard, and the experiences I had with the city all started to come together like a symphony. Each story and each experience its own instrument, and I was the conductor. I knew what had to be said and how to say it. My writing would remind people of the past and help them face their mistakes so they could move forward in a way that would accomplish the most good for the most people.

It's personal, political, and religious. As a journalist and storyteller, I had immersed myself in the stories of others. Gathering the breathings of their heart, I was there to disseminate the information in a way that could tip the needle of progress forward, even if just a bit. I was there to give a voice to the victims who have felt silenced by those richer and more powerful.

My story was about life post Katrina during hurricane season in New Orleans, but it was about so much more. It's about race and racism, class and classism, corruption, cover ups, and FEMA trailer toxicity.

Unsettled, I stared out the window, knowing I was longing for something, but not sure what. I turned to Theo and asked him if I was going to be okay. I hadn't been myself since I got home--he'd noticed it, I noticed it. I knew I wanted to be with Theo. I wasn't upset that he slept with a couple of people while I was gone. I didn't care. In fact, I was glad he'd had his physical needs met. Our sex life had been phenomenal since I returned.

"You are already okay, my love. You're just going through something right now. You'll get to the other side."

I had never understood the word swoon until Theo came into my life. Up to that point, swooning was just a concept. But the first time Theo gave me a journal because he saw it and thought of me, I felt the euphoria that is a swoon, first hand. His kindness toward my writing tantrum had the same effect to this day.

"How about you take a break and we go out for dinner?" Theo suggested, removing the half typed page from my now unclenched fist.

In the few weeks I had been home, our connection was growing stronger than ever. We had always loved each other deeply, but our relationship had never blossomed like this before. Maybe we were late bloomers, a concept Keira had recently reminded me of. A few days before I left New Orleans, she had mentioned that Quinn was a late bloomer with talking. "And all of a sudden, at 18 months old, she started speaking in full sentences," Keira told me proudly. Maybe Theo and I were late bloomers too, making up for lost time.

"Dinner sounds great. Where do you wanna go?" I asked Theo, entering a three-round match of "you pick" in which I lost. We ended up going food truck hopping because that's what I always pick if he makes me pick.

Before my trip, a simple decision like where to eat would take forever. We were simultaneously walking on eggshells and pushing one another's buttons. Our marriage vacation broke us of our old habits. Now, we showed each other more consideration and compassion. We didn't take things so seriously all the time. We stopped taking our relationship for granted. We were learning how to communicate all over again, but we were coming from a place of radical acceptance, and we offered each other endless grace. The part that shocks me the most to this day is the seemingly effortless way our new interactions were coming to both of us. For the first time in years, it was easy to love him and to feel loved by him.

I couldn't wrap my mind around the fact that I was resting my head on my Theo's shoulder after having committed what the church would call adultery, feeling more connected to my husband than I had been when I was a dutiful and chaste wife.

Being able to voice my desires in the bedroom without fear of judgment brought us both major satisfaction. I loved being able to talk to him about my fantasies, and in some cases, make them come true. I loved hearing about his desires, too, and making his fantasies come to life became one of mine.

Our connections outside of the bedroom deepened as well. We talked more freely about our dreams, him telling me about his desire to be a full time chef and me talking to him about my desire to write my memoir in the form of a novel.

Even our arguments were healthier. We listened more, got frustrated less, and apologized quicker.

How could this much joy in a relationship be against God's will? We weren't hurting anyone. There's no 50 Shades-ing going on in my bedroom. I mean, not until we're billionaires at least.

Chapter Thirty

THE HOLIDAYS

"You have everything you need?" Theo asked as I was packing my bag. That morning, we were heading to visit my hometown.

"I think so. I mean, I probably need more wine or Xanax," I joked.

I had started to find a groove back home in Austin. I'd joined a different yoga studio in hopes of meeting new people, picked up some freelance writing assignments, and had been working on my hurricane season piece. The article for which I'd spent six months gathering information was taking shape, and despite my earlier frustrations, the floodgates had graciously opened and the words poured out.

The holidays were fast approaching, which meant we were going home to visit family. I wasn't ready to make the drive to our hometown and see people who judged me for not being Christian enough when all they knew of me was I was pro-choice and LGBTQ affirming. I couldn't imagine the shame they would try to inflict upon me if they knew about my animated sex life and multiple partners. My parents would expect us to go to church on Christmas Eve, as was our tradition. As much as I didn't want to go, I knew that suffering through an adult contemporary praise team, a self-righteous sermon, and desperate plea for money would be easier than bucking the system with my parents. They were good people, just victims of the religious institution that permeated their community. I knew we would never see eye to eye on this, so I felt my lack of faith in mainstream Christianity was a subject better left untouched.

My mother, a retired emergency dispatcher, had a strong faith in Jesus and love for people. She showed everyone kindness and compassion no matter their age, race, creed, sexual orientation, or socioeconomic status, which is why it drove me crazy that she still voted against the marginalized. I couldn't understand the appeal of a little more money in the bank when it meant making life harder for so many of the people she seemed to care about.

I was raised to be polite before anything else, just like most of my white counterparts in the South, so tough conversations were off-limits. I wanted to challenge her, but my mom had been good to me, and I was worried about coming across as ungrateful. I knew she and my dad had done the best they could, despite their mistakes. I felt I needed my mom, and so I wasn't ready to challenge her to the point where our relationship could be threatened. I spent the 1.5 hour ride to my hometown doing guided meditation, hoping to assume a Zen-like state so as to remain unaffected by my family's stale religiosity.

Aside from a few rather unsavory remarks from my uncle, things at home were pretty peaceful. My mom was kind and welcoming, and she dutifully steered the conversations away from politics or religion. Even though I was the only non-evangelical, progressive believer in the house that week, my relatives run the gamut on religion. I had a Calvinist uncle and a charismatic aunt, and my cousins were atheist to fundamentalists and everywhere in between. I enjoyed talking to Kimmy, my Wiccan cousin, about my experience in New Orleans with Talia, the medium. I was careful to make sure my parents weren't around for any of these conversations, particularly the ones with my cousin Laine. Over a few glasses of spiked holiday punch, I opened up to her about my time in New Orleans. Even though we were close, I was still nervous about sharing openly, since she was part of my family. If they found out what I'd been up to, they would have a really hard time accepting me. Theo, on the other hand, had no problem opening up to Laine.

Even after describing the low points of New Orleans in depth, like the potholes, the crime, the wealth disparity, and the poor public school system, Laine was ready to move there.

"I don't know, it's all so captivating. Living in New Orleans sounds like living in a made up land. It sounds like a fairy tale or a fantasy."

"Hillary being in New Orleans was sort of a fairy tale." Theo said, giving out a clue that my trip was more than I had let on.

"What do you mean?" Laine looked over at me curiously.

Everything came pouring out. I told her all about my encounters in New Orleans, which was more information than Theo had previously heard. He and I had agreed we would keep the specifics of our separate sex lives to a minimum. While neither of us would be hurt necessarily, we figured the graphic details didn't need to be discussed. We could both tell the other had learned a thing or two in the bedroom, so it didn't matter who we had been with; it was Theo and I reaping the fruits of our labor--labor being code for "sex with others". Yet, there I was spilling my guts to Laine while Theo sat in silence, only to interject a couple of times reassuring Laine that yes, this is what we agreed to and yes, we were genuinely okay with our decision.

Sharing my story with someone who knew exactly how I had grown up felt so good. I longed to be the most "me" around the people who knew me best, but my family didn't give me much room to be my true self. For people who believe Christ accepts them in their imperfections, they certainly don't give that same level of acceptance to anyone else. Unless you naturally fit the mold, or contort yourself as close to it as possible, you are "prayed for" and "loved on" but not accepted. You don't get to be part of the community, but rather the community's pet project and/or object of ridicule. Even though I did my best to play the part, I was still ostracized and called a heretic by many in the church, simply because I accepted everyone as they were without any desire to change them.

Laine's acceptance meant the world to me, especially since she was raised in a more rigid home than I was. Her parents were in ministry, so the pressure to be perfect was suffocating for her and her four siblings. All of their normal childhood mistakes were up for scrutiny by the community, which meant their parents left them little room for error. It's no wonder all five of my cousins swung so far away from fundamentalism, they weren't even Christians anymore.

"Does this outfit look okay?" I asked Theo in mild desperation. I needed to look pretty, but not too pretty, for the Christmas Eve service. My maroon oversized sweater, black leggings, and the knee-high boots I borrowed from Keira were nothing anyone in New Orleans would raise an eyebrow over, but at my old church, if my outfit allowed anyone to see my curves in a sexual manner, I would surely feel their judgement. I was glad we had arrived a few minutes late so we didn't have to make small talk with anyone.

Laine and I got into a deep conversation about our upbringing as we sat in the pews waiting for the show to start.

"We couldn't question the leadership because we were told not to condemn God's anointed. Who said God anointed him, or anyone though? They are self-proclaimed anointed by God, which, in itself is an oxymoron, but that doesn't seem to bother the Christians I know. You can be as awful as you want to be, but if you're a straight man, particularly a straight white man and claim God called you to ministry, you become pretty much untouchable," Laine mused.

"I know. It's sickening, and it is past time for that toxic culture to change." I replied.

The service was showy and emotional, laden with contemporary worship songs and a high tech light show. Then came the solicitation. Looking around at the building with stadium seating, a coffee shop, bookstore and all the latest gadgets that said, "We're a church, but we're a cooooool church," I rolled my eyes at their plea for money. Why couldn't the pastor sell his boat or one of his cars to foot the bill for the upkeep of the giant church he decided to build?

I couldn't understand how the churchgoers didn't see they were being ripped off by someone who was clearly storing up treasures on earth rather than in heaven. I tried to keep a low-profile on the way out, saying little more than the quick, obligatory hello to those who saw me.

"Oh my gosh I'm so sorry!" In an effort to avoid eye-contact, I ended up running right into someone. I looked up to see Nathan, Megan's husband, staring at me.

"Heyyyyyy Hil!" he said, with a snarky glint in his eyes and a phony smile plastered on his face. I hated that he called me Hil. Only my real friends called me that.

I forced a smile through my pursed lips and gave him the traditional male/female Christian greeting, a side-hug. Even though I knew he was a not-great guy and even worse husband, I was relieved that he didn't seem to know his wife had stuck her tongue down my throat.

"Oh man, I'm sure Megan is going to be thrilled to see you." I had my doubts about that, but I kept my face neutral as Nathan continued. "She's grabbing the boys from children's church..." He went on to complain about children's church being too entertaining or something equally absurd. I was just glad she was momentarily occupied, so I could have a minute to compose myself before I saw her. In all the stress over my family, I hadn't considered the possibility of running into Megan at church. I knew she and her family had moved away for her job, but it never occurred to me that she, too, might be home for the holidays.

When Megan did make her way back to the sanctuary, kids in tow, I was sure she had been judged for her outfit. Donning a fitted green tank top that showed just a smidge of cleavage, her shoulders covered with a grey cardigan, a grey miniskirt, and black tights with black booties, she looked pretty hot. As she came toward us, I noticed a couple of glares thrown her way. I realized then that Megan was going through her own deconstruction. She must have been exhausted from being the good Christian all those years. Now, she was toeing the line when it came to her clothing, and she had made out with at least one person outside her marriage--and a woman, at that! I wished I could talk to her about things, but it was clearly neither the time nor place. The four of us: me, Theo, Megan, and her husband, exchanged small talk. Nathan dominated the conversation, not allowing Megan to get a word in, even as he talked about her. His demeaning comments were cut short when their toddler had to go potty and Megan excused herself. We took that opportunity to duck out of church, but not before Nathan called out, "How about the four of us do dinner while we're all in town?" Theo and I turned our heads back to him and nodded in agreement as we walked away.

"That dinner can never happen," I told Theo once we were in the car.

"Why not? Maybe you and Megan can put on a show for Nathan and me?" He teased.

I jokingly slapped his leg. "No way!"

We giggled like schoolchildren the whole ride back to my

parent's house. The rest of the visit was peaceful, culminating with our longstanding tradition of drinking too much champagne and popping off fireworks on New Year's Eve. We returned home, hoping a new year would bring a new sense of normalcy, but instead I only felt more unrest.

Chapter Thirty-One

SLEEPLESS NIGHTS

"I WISH YOU KNEW ALL THAT WAS WEIGHING ON ME." I SAID quietly to Theo, knowing he couldn't hear me.

It was late one cold January night, and Theo was fast asleep. I lay next to him, feeling the warmth from his body. He was always warm, even with the unusually chilly temps we were having in Austin. My guided meditation wasn't working; my mind was unable to rest. I couldn't sleep. I slipped carefully out of bed, grabbed my laptop, draped a throw blanket over my shoulders, and made myself comfortable on our living room couch. My thoughts began to swirl.

What is wrong with me? I have everything I want. My marriage is better than I ever hoped. Sex is fun now; I have no regrets. I don't feel shame. I don't think God is judging me, but I miss spirituality. I miss feeling close to Jesus, but even my progressive, affirming church wouldn't approve of my life. I don't need their approval, so why do I crave it? Why do I feel the need for my Christian friends to agree that my sex life does not determine how "Christian" I am? Why do I crave validation from my church community? I'm committed to loving Jesus, loving others, and social justice. I care about the broken and the hurting; yet I can't shake the fear of judgment. These people raised me, taught me... allegedly loved me. Would they really cast me aside like stale bread because I dared to explore my own sexuality? I'm still struggling to separate myself from my roots. I feel like I'm constantly looking over my shoulder, having to watch what I say and who I say it to. I'm so glad to be home with Theo, but I am not at peace. I thought I would be more together by now. I've been home almost two months. Shouldn't I have more resolution by now? Is there a part of me that feels guilty for what I did? I don't think so. What was the result of my so-called sexual impurity? I found a great friend in Keira. My relationship with my husband is flourishing. I am confident. My sex life is healthy. I am no longer ashamed of my body. I resolved 10-year-old feelings with Jacob. Isn't that good? Why would God condemn me?

In the book of John, when the woman caught in adultery was brought to Jesus, he did not condemn her. He spoke truth to those who accused her, telling them "Let he who is without sin cast the first stone." We humans are in no place to cast stones, and Jesus himself does not condemn her, therefore, I refuse to accept the condemnation which will be thrust upon me by my church community if they ever find out who I really am.

In the wee hours of the morning, when daylight first broke through the window, Theo rolled over and asked, "Have you been up all night, hon?"

"I have. I'm trying to write through all these feelings." I told him. I was so glad we could be so open with each other. Before, I would have been worried about telling him I stayed up all night, thinking he would be upset that I didn't get any rest.

"You've had a lot of sleepless nights since you've been home.

Are you sure there's nothing else going on?" I could tell he was concerned. I was, too.

"I'm sure. I mean, something is obviously going on, but I can't figure out what yet. I know I'm working through a lot of feelings still, and though I've come a long way, I still have miles to go before I will be whole."

I made us a pot of coffee and we sat down to drink it before he had to get ready for work.

"Is there anything you want to talk about?" Theo asked me once we sat down, coffee mugs in hand.

"Yes and no. I am no longer filled with shame, but I do have an irrational fear of judgement from my family and home-town community. Part of me wants to tell our story--the unabridged, X-rated version--so people like Megan can feel less alone in their struggles. Another part of me shudders at the thought of anyone knowing what I've done."

Theo reminded me that my life is mine to live, and my target audience is me. He helped me see that I can tell all or part of my story however and whenever I want to. He used a lot of eloquent, supportive words, but the best thing he said to me that morning was, "Fuck 'em."

"If people don't accept you for who you are, fuck 'em. They're not your people."

And with that, I began to find the intrinsic motivation I needed to keep moving forward.

Chapter Thirty-Two

JUST SEX

"THANK YOU FOR YOUR EMAIL. I WILL BE OUT OF THE OFFICE the next 48 hours, and will reply as soon as possible."

I set my out of office reply on my email and spent the day at the spa. I couldn't get my head clear, and although it wasn't the most judicious use of money I thought some good old fashioned pampering would get me out of this funk. I booked a manicure, pedicure, facial, detox bath, and massage.

After my facial, it was time to soak in the deep, hot bath one of the staff members had drawn for me. "Don't forget to drink water," she said, motioning to the glass of lemon water on the side of the tub.

I stepped inside and slowly lowered my body into the tub. Steam was coming off the water, but I didn't mind. I relished hot baths, in contrast to Theo, who preferred cold showers. I always wished we could have sex in the shower, but we couldn't agree on the water temperature. Either he was burning up or I was freezing cold. "I bet we could fit in this

tub together," I thought. My body started to get tingly. Even
though the door was locked, I was a little nervous. Until I
had started thinking about sex, I had been the most relaxed
I'd been in months. I decided to take care of myself in hopes
of returning to the relaxed state I'd been in before my mind
started to imagine Theo and I having sex in the tub.

"How was your bath?" asked the massage therapist, who
looked like he could have been a bouncer at a club. He introduced himself as Stephan and told me to undress to my
level of comfort. After he put on soft music and left the
room, I did just that--I stripped completely naked. This was
a big change for me, as I used to always leave my bra and
panties on during massages. As I laid there looking up at the
tile ceiling, covered only by a thin blanket, I felt good about
how comfortable I had become in my own skin.

Stephan began by rubbing my shoulders, then worked
down to the small of my back. As his hands moved lower,
my body responded with arousal. Despite having had an
orgasm in the tub 30 minutes earlier, I was filled with desire
again. Immediately, pangs of guilt hit me, and I attempted to
squelch my lustful thoughts. "My marriage is no longer
open. Why am I thinking about sex right now?" Suddenly,
something shifted in my thinking and I realized I had
nothing to feel guilty about. Feeling sexy when someone is
massaging you isn't wrong. I had no plans to solicit Stephen
for sex. I wasn't even thinking about having sex *with him*. My
body was just responding to external stimuli. I wasn't doing
anything wrong. All of my married Christian friends got
massages. They seemed to think it was perfectly acceptable
to have a stranger rub their hands all over their naked
bodies. Why was it such a big deal when sex was involved?
It's just sex.

"And that's when I figured out what sex was!" I exclaimed emphatically to Theo, after recounting my experience at the spa.

"Yeah, why are we okay with all kinds of other connections but if there's an orgasm involved it's taboo?" Theo had a good point. By that time, quite a few other people caused me to experience the pleasure of an orgasm, and I didn't feel any more or less connected to them, or to Theo, because of it. He and Stephan both massaged my back, but I still loved Theo and had little to no feelings for the massage therapist.

It's just sex. Sex was only a big deal because the adults in my life made it so. It is just sex. A biological and evolutionary mechanism which ensures our species' survival. Are there emotions tied to it? I have no emotional attachment to the bartender, to Will, and certainly none toward Bennett. It was only after having sex that Jacob and I were able to untether our emotional connection. At the same time, I have better sex with Theo because of our closeness, and the same is true for Keira.

Sex is like going down a waterslide. The anticipation builds with each step. The longer you sit on the ledge before you go down, the bigger the thrill. Sex was designed to be enjoyed. If our therapist Betsy was right, sex was designed for women to enjoy for enjoyment's sake. But sex isn't more than trust. It isn't more than respect. It isn't more than laughter. Sex isn't more special than any other aspect of a deep relationship.

My friend Alex and I both love tennis. Theo hates tennis, so I play with Alex. It doesn't mean I love Theo any less. Alex and I both play the same kind of "lazy girl" tennis, so she and I share that connection. I don't think sex and tennis are the same thing, but no metaphor is perfect. As far back as I can remember, sex has been elevated to an unrealistic level. Sex was simultaneously part of my purpose in life, to please my husband and help with his spiritual growth, and the one thing that could wreck me for eternity if it happened before someone slipped a ring on my finger and signed a piece of paper. I was amazed at what one day at the spa had revealed to me.

"I'm not sure Quinn and I can come to Austin for Mardi Gras." Keira's text was a gut punch. I missed her. I wanted to see her and show her where I lived. I was also curious how the three of us would get along. I was optimistic, but not entirely certain that there wouldn't be any awkwardness. Hearing that she might not be coming after all had me fighting back tears. I could see she was still typing, so I held off on replying.

"Brad is being such a jackass," she continued. "He doesn't want Quinn to miss Endymion, and since that's the Saturday before Mardi Gras, it would cut right through our trip plans."

I understood what she meant, but not fully. I had forgotten Mardi Gras was more than just a day. Since I always wanted to experience it, I thought maybe this would be a good time to take Theo to New Orleans. I texted Keira back: "What if Theo and I came to visit you?" A few minutes later my phone chirped. I smiled from ear to ear upon seeing her emphatic "Omg, YES" reply.

Theo was more than happy to go, and I was thrilled about this change in plans. I would still get to see Keira *and* experience New Orleans with Theo during what promised to be the city's most epic celebration.

Chapter Thirty-Three

MARDI GRAS

"THROW ME SOMETHING, MISTER!" I HAD NO IDEA HOW MUCH I would hear those words during Mardi Gras. Revelry, beads, glitter, and camaraderie all flowed through the streets of New Orleans the week we spent visiting Keira.

I learned a lot I hadn't previously known about Mardi Gras during my first visit. For example:

- You can't park anywhere near the parades for several hours before they start.
- Post parade parties are a thing.
- Elderly people will step on your hand to get "their" doubloons.
- King Cake comes in a variety of types, most of which are delicious.
- Mardi Gras is a *mostly* family friendly atmosphere.
- Only tourists show their breasts for beads.
- Mardi Gras is a time to let go of your inhibitions and give in to debauchery.

The city was the same as when I called it home, but even more alive. The trees along the parade routes were decorated with colorful plastic beads. Everyone had a spring in their step, probably from all the king cakes eaten at breakfast over the course of Carnival season.

Most of all, I was happy to be spending time with Keira. I hadn't seen her in almost three months, and though we'd only met nine months prior, she was closer to me than many of my lifelong friends.

Theo explored the city solo one afternoon, discovering firsthand that a Tuesday in New Orleans is better than a Saturday pretty much anywhere else, leaving Keira and me to catch up.

"I really miss it here," I confessed. "I didn't realize how much until now."

"Well, I miss having you here." Keira told me. She looked amazing. I knew she'd started working out, but I didn't realize that it would put her already-nice physique into smoking-hot territory.

When I read her what I had of my Hurricane Season piece, she cried. "Mission accomplished" I said, trying to lighten the suddenly somber mood.

When I decided to write the piece, I'd wanted to reach down into the soul of the city and capture what the people endured and still endure. I wanted to call attention to the plight of the un/der insured, the people who lost their lives or the lives of their loved ones, and those who were facing illness thanks to their extended stays in FEMA trailers. I wanted to show the strength and class of a group who, when faced with an unprecedented catastrophe, showed remarkable grace and resilience. I wanted to show that nothing, not mother nature's fury nor our government's shortcomings, could destroy the spirit of New Orleans. If Keira's tears told me anything, it was that I had done what I set out to do.

Keira asked me where I would publish the article. I didn't know. I was scared to put myself out there. Did I have any right to tell this story when I didn't live it? I don't have first-hand memories of area wide curfews and government issued Meal Ready-to-Eat, or MRE's as interviewees called them.

"But you can tap into other people's pain like no one I've ever seen," Keira assured me. "Even though you don't have kids, you can relate to my mom stories more than any child-free person I know. You may not have lived through Katrina, but you have experienced it through the people you interviewed. You are sharing their pain, their triumph. You are the vessel which the story moves through. You can give voice to this story, even if it isn't your story to tell."

She was seriously a gift from God. Or the universe. Keira didn't make much of a fuss over herself, but she was a force to be reckoned with. Her wisdom and wit were comforting and reassuring. I considered myself lucky to have someone like her in my corner, cheering me on. The only other person I had in my life who was truly supportive of me was Theo.

"Our visit was too short," I complained, noticing my pants were a bit snug after spending seven days eating more fried chicken and king cake than I thought humanly possible.

"Our visit wasn't sexy enough," Theo shot back.

"We should have talked about it beforehand. I wanted to, but I didn't know how to broach the subject. I was hoping you would take the lead there," I confessed.

"Yeah, because I can take the lead in trying to have sex with my wife and her best friend." Theo's words were dripping with sarcasm.

"She really is my best friend. I don't think I've had one before, aside from you, of course. But yes, you could have taken the lead and we probably would've had sex. Instead, we watched movies."

I would have loved another chance to be with Theo and Keira. About a week after we returned to Austin, I mustered the courage to mention it to Keira.

"You know... I couldn't help but wonder about the three of us when we were visiting," I texted her hesitantly.

"Wonder about what? Us getting together?" She texted back.

"Yes, but like, *together* together." I replied.

"I knew what you meant. I wondered, too. In fact, I kind of hoped," she confessed.

At that moment, I wished I could turn time back to the Sunday night of our visit, when Quinn was with her dad and the three of us had gone to a parade earlier in the day along with a few of Keira's friends. Back at Keira's house, we poured some wine and sat on her porch, listening to the dying sounds of the marching bands as the second parade of the evening, which we'd opted to skip, neared the end of their route.

Later that night, our conversation had turned a little flirta-tious, but we ended the evening abruptly, all of us citing tiredness. I could see, looking back, that the moment had presented itself to us, but we had stepped back from it instead of leaning in.

Rather than obsess over the sex we'd all missed out on, I decided to put it out of my mind and focus on figuring out who I was and what I really wanted. After being back in Austin for over three months, I still had no idea.

I didn't connect with my Christian friends at all anymore, not even my progressive ones. Sure, they were forward-thinking Christians; they voted blue and gave out free Mom hugs at Pride Parades, but were they going to understand the fact that I would be totally cool with inviting another woman into our marital bed a first time, much less a second? I couldn't find the courage to risk that, so I closed part of myself off from some of the people who knew me best. My evangelical friends from my hometown barely knew how different my church was from theirs, and they certainly didn't know about my lack of belief in eternal hell or my disillusionment with the entire Christian religion.

I was feeling pretty alone even though I kept myself busy, picking up as many freelance writing assignments as possi-ble, which also helped me procrastinate publishing my piece on Hurricane Season.

I wanted the article to be perfect, so I kept revising it. I didn't want to submit it just anywhere; I wanted to get it to a publi-cation that would reach the people who needed to read it most. I wanted that piece to cause readers to experience both empathy and awe toward the people of New Orleans. Keira's encouragement helped more than she knew, but I still had a long way to go if I was going to be brave enough to publish one of my most treasured works. Even though the Katrina story wasn't about me, had I bared my soul in the article.

Chapter Thirty-Four

GETTING AWAY

"WHAT DO YOU THINK?" I ASKED THEO, HOLDING UP A handcrafted earring to my ear.

Spring had sprung. The bluebonnets were blooming, bike riders were cruising around the city, and restaurants opened their patios for al fresco dining. It was my favorite time of year in Austin: festival season. Nothing brings me joy quite like an outdoor festival. I love seeing people proudly display their work. I love talking to the vendors about their creations. I once saw a woman who designed beautiful jewelry using chain mail, I bought a skateboard that is a true work of art, and I've had the best chocolate chip cookie of my life at a festival. Being able to tell the baker it was my favorite made my heart happy. Except this year, my heart was restless and my mind was unsettled. I thought surely I would be out of this funk by now. I couldn't figure out why I wanted out of my own skin so much.

"Why don't we go away next weekend? Just to camp at Lake Travis," Theo suggested while we strolled in and out of booths. Getting away sounded nice. "Maybe I need a change of scenery," I thought to myself. Being in New Orleans over Mardi Gras had cheered me up for a while; maybe a weekend at the lake would do the same.

"I love that idea," I said to Theo, wrapping my arms around his neck and leaning in for a quick kiss.

The next weekend, we headed about an hour west to Pace Bend Park. Before we left, I could feel my mood lifting. Whatever dark cloud that had been with me almost constantly since I returned from New Orleans was breaking and the sun was shining through. Theo and I had camped semi-regularly over the years, but this time we were going to do something I had never done before. We were going to eat mushrooms.

Aside from the occasional puff from a joint or the few times I tried THC edibles, I wasn't much of a drug user. I didn't drink often, and even when I needed them, I typically refused narcotic pain-killers because they made my stomach hurt. But once I started reading the scientific research behind psilocybin, the active ingredient in magic mushrooms, I became curious enough to give it a whirl. There are no reported overdoses, accidental or otherwise, therefore they are safer than the Vicodin my doctor prescribed to me for kidney stones.

After we got everything set up, Theo, being the ever-practical and logical guy he was, made sure we had full cell phone batteries and the portable hotspot was charged in case we needed the internet to look for a nearby hospital. These precautions were mainly for my benefit, in case I freaked out. Theo was no stranger to hallucinogens. He was a raver kid in his youth, so he had tried his fair share of drugs. He grew out of the phase as a young adult shortly before meeting me, but he still indulged from time to time. He was always an advocate for natural mind-altering substances. He said they made him feel closer to God, nature, and himself. Despite my conditioning, I was never strongly opposed to drugs like marijuana and mushrooms.

During the almost four months I had been home, I had not felt comfortable. The best way I could describe it is the way I felt when I gained 15 pounds yet forced myself into my same clothes in an effort to avoid buying a new wardrobe. Everything felt uncomfortable. Too tight. After living in New Orleans, I was more myself than ever, yet less comfortable in my skin than before I left.

After going through so much to free myself from the years of shame and self-loathing that had been bestowed upon me by my church and reinforced by my (well-meaning) parents, I was ready to try something new. I thought maybe if I could get myself to a state of mind where I could "smell colors" the way Theo described, maybe I could identify and shake off whatever had been bothering me.

"Shouldn't I feel something by now?" I asked Theo.

"Maybe. I'm feeling it a little, but it affects everyone differently," he replied. That was our last sober conversation of the night.

All of a sudden, my mind went silent. The constant buzzing of fear, worry, doubt, and shame that plagued my thoughts came to a grinding halt. Rather than being alarmed by this, I was calm. Worry no longer existed. I sat staring at the vibrant colors around me, the trees greener than when we arrived. My heart smiled and I rested in total contentment.

I expected to be drawn out of reality; instead, I was drawn

inward, to the core of who I was. My external life faded away and only the present mattered. Theo and I walked hand in hand to the lake where we sat at the shoreline, looking out at the water, watching the clouds change shape and the sky turn from light blue to varying shades of pink and orange as the sun began to set.

"I feel beautiful," Theo said. I snapped a picture of him and told him that he should because he was beautiful.

"My mind... It's so quiet. Is this what peace feels like?" I wondered aloud.

That night, I contemplated the beauty and wonder of our smallness, and felt the magnitude of our greatness. I saw life as a continuum. An ever-evolving tapestry of existence. I understood that I am connected to my ancestors and my future offspring as much as I am connected to my friends and to strangers and to the earth. We are all separate, but we are all one.

"All that from a tiny bit of mushrooms?" Theo asked, surprised. He said he knew they would help me. I wish I had tried them sooner.

"I guess what I'm saying is, I don't want to be afraid or ashamed of who I am anymore. I'm tired of holding my tongue and backing down because I'm scared of what my family and friends might think. I want to live my life out loud without worrying about their condemnation. Maybe I should open up about everything. Maybe people need to hear that it's possible to have threesomes and extra-marital sex yet while still being madly in love and wanting to grow old with your spouse. Maybe they need to hear that women can take control of their lives and sexuality, and a strong man will give them the space they need in which to do it."

"Yeah, but not everybody needs that extreme of an adventure," Theo replied, thinking practically again.

"I know, and that's beside the point," I replied. "The actions don't need to be identical. People can find their own way. They can open their minds and allow themselves to explore."

"So, what do you want to do?" Theo asked, genuinely unsure where I was going with my sudden enlightenment.

"I don't know, really." I thought about making a social media post affirming pre-marital sex, but other than that I had no idea. When we returned home from camping, I was determined to figure out a way to share my truth.

Chapter Thirty-Five

OTHER WOMEN

A FEW WEEKS AFTER MY ENLIGHTENING EXPERIENCE WITH magic mushrooms, I was still mulling over the idea of going public. I created a social media account under a pseudonym and began posting about the hypocrisy I saw in the church. I started a website where I chronicled my evangelical upbringing and my journey into heresy.

It turned out, I wasn't alone. I found many other women who grew up entrenched in purity culture. We were all different in our relationships and sexuality: some had transitioned, some married their first loves and were now divorced; some still happily married; some of them were dating other women who grew up in the same subculture. We all lived similar childhoods. We all felt similar shame and self-loathing around sex. We all wanted to talk about our stories, but had been conditioned to keep silent about anything related to s-e-x.

Thanks to the hashtag #ExChristian, I met some new friends, most notably, Carmen. Carmen from the Midwest and grew up in an extreme version of evangelicalism. Her dad was a pastor and her mom ran the children's ministry. She was home-schooled until her dad's church added a private school, and there, she was taught from a fundamentalist curriculum.

Carmen seemed to understand me better than I understood myself. She graciously took me under her wing, acting as a sort of mentor.

"I was you once," she told me. "I went through the same realizations; the same grief. I suffered the loss of lifelong friends and family members. My circle of support-- the support I thought was unconditional and based on grace-- was absolutely conditional and based in a narrow set of arbitrary rules."

As the summer rolled around and the temperatures began to rise, I found myself coming completely unglued.

"This isn't supposed to be my life!!" I railed and raged into the phone, screaming my head off to Carmen. "I should have loved myself all along!!" I shrieked. Through sobs and sniffles, I told the little girl who lives inside me, the one I grew up hating, that it was okay. That she was okay. She wasn't broken. She wasn't evil. She was good. The people in charge of her were the evil ones. Whether they knew it or not, they had stolen her childhood; her innocence, her confidence. They almost robbed her of her future.

"It's okay, Hillary. You have plenty of time to right their wrongs. I'm almost 36, which is basically ancient compared to you. I was 33 when I hit the place you are now in my deconstruction. This is your low, babe. You are only going to go up from here." Carmen's reassuring words helped dry my tears and slow my breathing.

Though I wanted to believe her, it was impossible to imagine I would ever get to a place of true healing. The house of cards that was my faith started shaking before I got married, when Deena, a friend from youth group, publicly renounced Christianity. Until that point, I had only seen people go from unsaved to saved. How and why would anyone want to leave our religion? My problems with the Christian church's teachings worsened once I got married and started having sex. I didn't know what sex was. I didn't know how to have sex. I didn't know much about my body or Theo's. Our first time was awkward, despite how much I loved him. I couldn't relax. I couldn't get turned on because getting turned on wasn't a thing I had ever allowed myself to do before. Theo was so patient. Kissing me softly, complimenting my body, telling me how much he loved me. But all I wanted to do was taste the once forbidden fruit. I wanted to experience the reward for keeping myself pure and only having sex within its proper context of marriage. Only, I was stiff and dry and ashamed. Theo stopped. He didn't like the way I was acting. He said it didn't seem like consent.

"What do you mean? You feel like you're doing this against my will?" I asked, frustrated and confused.

"No, not exactly. But you don't seem like you want to." Theo said gently. I could tell that he too was frustrated, which made me feel even worse.

"Well, I want to," I huffed. "Isn't the fact that I'm married to you and laying naked on the bed evidence enough?" I was not good with my words when I felt overcome with shame.

Eventually, we did it. Theo was gentle, but all I felt was discomfort. I cried after my first time. Over the last few years, I'd shed thousands of tears around sex and sexuality.

The thing that was supposed to bring me joy, fulfillment, and connection almost cost me my marriage, and moving away from the religion that destroyed me was now threatening to destroy several of my relationships.

Even though I had made it through Christmas at home without any drama, my family life was strained. I couldn't talk to my mom like I used to. Her only advice was "I'll pray for you" or "God will work it out." Those had become all but empty words. I don't know what God is or if s/he hears our prayers. I can't imagine God hearing the prayers of a desperate mother, clinging to her baby's dying breath and saying, "Sorry, but my plan was for him to die at birth." Yes, good things are born out of tragedy. Maybe the mom who lost her son goes on to find a cure for the disease which robbed her of her ability to be a mother, but if God is so powerful, couldn't he just create her with the knowledge and desire to cure that disease instead of making her bury her baby?

My marriage was thriving, but outside of it I was desperately alone. The God I once knew was no longer recognizable. I could not bring myself to believe in the God of the Bible, no matter how hard I tried. I wanted to make a public statement the way Deena did all those years ago. I typed these words into my blog:

Dear Friends,

I have something I need to share. First, I want to say I am thankful for everyone in my circle. I love you all so much. As the years have passed, I have transformed. I no longer ascribe to many of my closely held beliefs, including those of the modern day Evangelical church. This is not to say I don't believe in God, but I do not see the Jesus I read about in the scriptures represented in American Christianity. The church has closed its doors to the hurting, to the ones whom Jesus welcomed with open arms. The evangelical church's moral condemnation of the LGBTQ+ community, their opposition to women's bodily autonomy, their quest for political power, and their acceptance of sexual abusers are in direct opposition to the teachings of the God they claim to serve. While I am moving away from Christianity, I do not question my salvation. I am not lost. I did not backslide. My desire to do justly, love mercy, and walk humbly is what pushed me away from the church.

Then, I stopped typing, saved the draft, and never published the post. My fears got the best of me. It wasn't a total waste, though. Writing the words out, even if they were only for my eyes, brought me a healthy dose of liberation. I was beginning to understand who I wasn't: a sinner, and what I didn't believe: in the teachings of evangelical Christianity. But who was I, and what did I believe? Only time would teach me.

Chapter Thirty-Six

NEW NAME

"Who created God?" Six-year-old me asked my mom.

When I was a little girl, I had no problem asking questions or speaking truth. I asked my mom how God could always be there. She told me he just was. I asked how he could possibly know everything. She almost always said, "God's ways are higher than our ways."

I asked friends, family, and church leaders big, heavy questions about creation, salvation, life, and death only to have them deflected, ignored, and in some cases, rebuked. Somewhere along the way, after having my questions placated, ignored, or even shut down in anger, I stopped asking. I stopped speaking out. I couldn't reconcile all the atrocities I was seeing in the world with Christians claiming God answered their prayer to stop the rain so they could go fishing. I couldn't understand people who praised God for "blessing them" with a brand new, luxury car when kids in my neighborhood went to bed hungry some nights.

I wondered why such a wealthy church didn't use its abundance to help answer the prayers of those in need. Instead, they built new buildings, and the staff, along with some members of the congregation, showed off their material possessions as if they were a visible sign of God's blessing. How about white Evangelicals dole out some of the grace they claim God has bestowed upon the world, instead of showing contempt for people who don't fit the narrow, homogenous mold? I wanted to speak out, but fear got the best of me. The church was my community. My home. I couldn't set fire to my own home and not expect to get burned. One late-spring Austin evening after I returned home from New Orleans, I had an opportunity to be brave and speak out against the ever-present Evangelical Christian hypocrisy. I came across an article online where a woman shared the reasons for her divorce. She claimed her love for her kids and their well-being is what compelled her to leave her husband. In the article, she professed her love for God and for the Bible, but went on to explain that her marriage was toxic, and she knew getting out was the best thing she could do for her children. And then I read the comments.

"This is garbage! Why even get married then? God does not put people together until they're not happy anymore. It's a commitment for life- it's in the vows you make to one another. This teaches children it's ok to quit the hard stuff in life and to seek happiness at the cost of others," a vicious commenter posted.

" '...sometimes God brings people together for a time, but not forever.' No, that's not how God works. Not in marriage," another commenter said, quoting the article simply to disagree with it.

"What happened to 'til death do us part?' You make a promise before God to spend your life with that person. I don't see how it is beneficial to your children to see their parents splitting up. You have to learn to work things out. This kind of thing has ruined the sanctity of marriage," another one read.

The women who left those vitriolic comments were clearly against divorce, but what really seemed to bother them was that the author didn't seem repentant about her decision. They didn't like that she was planning to be happy after leaving an unhealthy relationship.

"Doesn't Jesus say the most important rule is to love God and love others?" I asked them directly. I suggested they stop beating people with the Bible and reminded them of a quote from their savior:

"Let him who is without sin cast the first stone." –Jesus

I had had enough. I did not care if I lost friends for standing up for what is right.

By the time spring was in full effect in Austin, I was done with the version of Christianity I grew up in, but I was more spiritual than I had been my whole life. Thinking back on my time in New Orleans, I could see clearly just how connected to the divine I felt there. My experiences back in Austin, even with my wonderful, progressive church, paled in comparison to the times in NOLA where I felt the depth and breadth of Divinity's love. Call it God, Source, Guide, Higher Self-- the name doesn't matter. After all, a rose by any other name would smell just as sweet.

I could no longer tolerate people who used the name of Jesus to rain down judgement and shame upon others. The stone-throwing comments were the final straw. We couldn't possibly share the same faith. Either they were Christians or I was. I knew I was, so they can be the ones to get a new name.

I'm still a Christian. Despite everything I have gone through, I still believe in the life and work of Jesus. I love the creative force behind us, and I love creation. I am a Christian. Those who judge people's relationship with God based on trivial things like their sexual orientation or views on abortion can take a seat. They will not rob me of this name. They are the ones who gave up the teachings of Jesus in exchange for a version of Christianity that only seems to care about unborn American children, all while expecting those children to pull themselves up by their bootstraps the second they exit the womb. The people who vote against social services, who kick others when they are down and who carry an air of moral superiority about them, they can be the ones to give up the title of Christian.

I am a Christian. I am married. I am bisexual. I am good. I am holy. I am free. I am loved by the creator. I am a valuable member of the body of Christ, just like every other person who lives the life of a Jesus follower. Our sexuality has no bearing on our faithfulness.

Those who sit in judgement, who think they can decide who is and isn't part of the group, they are the ones who can get a new name. I am a Christian.

I am a Christian who doesn't believe Jesus is the only way. I know what he said. I know the scripture. *"I am the way, the truth, and the life. No one comes to the Father except through Me."* To interpret these words to mean that only people who hear about Jesus and his life, death, and resurrection are the only ones who could ever enter heaven is to believe that entire generations and civilizations, no matter how much they connected with the divine, would be cast aside, and the pastors who rape women in the congregation are fine because they say they believe in Jesus. Jesus said, "By their fruit you will recognize them." The fruit I've seen from mainstream, evangelical Christianity is poisonous and, if we're listening to Jesus, the tree should be cut down and thrown into the fire.

They cannot take Christianity from me. I. Am. A. Christian.

I love the Lord my God with all my heart, soul, mind and strength. I love my neighbor as I love myself. And I do love myself. I am beautiful and whole and pure. I accept myself, both my flaws and my strengths, knowing neither define me. I am worthy because I am. If the mainstream Christians don't like this, then they can be the ones to get a new name. I am a Christian.

I typed those words onto the internet. Of course, no one saw them because I did not share them with my network. I just posted them to a blog, under my name, and knowing they were "out there" caused my heart to pound, both in trepidation and exhilaration. I had come so far, yet was still concerned about the judgement from my community. At the same time, sharing my truth, even only 478 words of my truth, gave me courage to keep telling my story.

I thought about the words of Talia, the medium I met. "You have a gift, my child. Share your gift of storytelling with those who need it."

I knew I wasn't alone in my feelings. I knew I wasn't the only woman damaged by purity culture. I knew I wasn't the only person whose religious beliefs were in flux. I hoped my story, or at least, a portion of my story, could help people struggling with their evangelical upbringing.

Chapter Thirty-Seven

SHOTGUN DOUBLE

"I miss you," I texted Keira.

I had been back in Austin for over five months. My marriage was strong. Theo and I could talk to one another about anything. The walls that once lined my heart had crumbled when I was in New Orleans. I became the person I was meant to be, a person who loves big and true. A person who is no longer afraid of judgement, shame, or rejection. At least, not in my marriage. But something wasn't right. I no longer fit in my old life.

I still feared the judgement of everyone around me, especially those who knew the old me. Since extramarital sex is uncommon in our society, I worried about my Christians and non-Christian friends alike, but my experiences would be especially judge-worthy to my Christian friends; the ones who have claimed authority as the only people who know Jesus. But I know the real Jesus. The one who ached for the hurting and cared more about people than laws. The one who called the hypocrites on their shit. If Jesus walked the earth today the way he did over 2000 years ago, he would be condemning American Christianity and their unholy union to political power. Why did I care so much what they thought? Because the church told me they could decide my fate. They had me believing they were the only ones who could decide if I was a "real" Christian or not. But they can't. They have no authority over my salvation or my Christianity.

I feel for my friends like Megan who are trapped in a life they wish they could leave. Megan keeps her desires hidden so that she can remain within the culture she needs. I encourage her, and all the Megan's of the world, to live in their truth. You'll find friends, and dare I say family, when you live an authentic life.

I will no longer be afraid to put myself out there. I will tell my story. Because people need to know they aren't alone. They need to know it is possible to leave their past behind and live the life they were born to live. These days, I can proudly say I am doing the same.

I'm sitting on *my* front porch swing. Writing this from *my* shotgun double.

The end.

Chapter Thirty-Eight
THE MORE

OKAY, LOOK. I DIDN'T WANT TO DO THAT TO YOU. BUT THAT'S how memoirs always seem to end. I know, because I've read a ton of them. You're always left wanting more or saying, "And that's it? You sat on a bench eating ice cream?" Tell me more! So, this is the more I hope you're craving right now.

Almost a year to the day after I left for New Orleans, Theo sat me down for what seemed like a serious, "I want a divorce" kind of talk.

"Hillary, you are not happy here," he told me. Theo could be brutally honest sometimes, but it always came from a place of love. He was telling me something I was scared to admit. I kept saying I was uncomfortable, which was true, but I was in denial until this fateful day.

"I'm sorry. I want to be. I love you. I don't want to be without you." I broke down. "But you're right, I'm not happy." I was ugly-crying by this point.

"It's okay. It's okay," Theo assured me, wrapping his arms

around me from behind, allowing me to lean back into his chest.

My heart slowed and my body started to relax, as I knew he would hold me up. Theo had been holding me up ever since we got together. I loved it. I appreciated it. But I wanted to stand on my own. I couldn't do that in Austin. In that setting, my conditioning took over. My fears got the best of me. I couldn't stand in my truth.

I sniffled and used my shirt to dry my eyes before telling Theo, "I saw a John Goodman quote online the other day. It said something about how he came to New Orleans a long time ago and how there's an incomplete part of our chromosomes that gets repaired or found when we hit New Orleans. He thinks some of us just belong there."

Theo stared at me uncomprehendingly.

"And I know what he means," I continued. "I know what it means to miss New Orleans... and I want to move back." I didn't fully realize that's what I wanted until I uttered the words aloud.

"I want you to come with me. But only if you really want to. I love you, Theo, and I want to spend my life with you, but I don't fit here anymore, and I have to leave so that I can thrive. I'm dying here. And my heart is longing to go back. Saving our marriage was the reason I went in the first place, but in order to save myself, I need to go back. I hope you'll come with me."

"Is it really a good idea to just up and move? I mean, we have jobs." Most of the time, I loved and needed Theo's practicality, but sometimes, I wished he would just take the dang leap instead of trying to map out all the steps.

"Theo, we can work from anywhere. But if you don't want to, don't. I would rather you stay here than go for me. I have to go, though. I can't live like this anymore." I earnestly plead my case.

"Do you really think moving will help? Aren't we far enough away from your community already?" Theo asked.

"It's not just about proximity to my community, but being so close to them means we're expected for holidays, and I don't like having the conflict with my family about not going. If we live out of state, we only have to come back maybe once or twice a year. It's more than that, though." I told him.

We sat in silence for a while, each of us trying to process the magnitude of our discussion. Was our better-than-ever marriage about to end? Were we moving to New Orleans? Would I go alone? Did my efforts to save my marriage lead to its destruction?

"I don't know me. I lived in and around here all my life, so I constantly see reminders of who I used to be. And I didn't love that person. I didn't even like that person. I want to go somewhere I can know myself, be myself, and love myself," I said.

"I'd love to watch you love yourself," Theo quipped. He was always one for joking at inopportune times. Sometimes, he was able to lighten the mood. Other times, he'd make it worse. This time, I chuckled a bit because I had really walked right into that one.

"Let's go," he said. "I can think of a million reasons why it's a bad idea, but it could also be pretty damn amazing. I want to be with you. The you I saw in New Orleans. You are fully and completely you there. You deserve to live freely. I'm fine here, but I don't love Austin the way you love New Orleans."

My heart nearly leapt out of my chest. New Orleans, in its perfectly imperfect way, got me. I learned how to be myself in that city, and could not wait to call it home.

A few months later, Theo and I moved into a shotgun double, similar to the one in Bayou St. John, only this time in an area known as Mid-City, where we are living happily ever after. Or at least, ever after. Just like all of life, happiness comes and goes. As for my relationship with God, it's more than I could have asked for. I live a life of true freedom and boundless grace. As for the future, who knows? What I've learned over this time of self-exploration is that life is too fluid to be put in a box. Sometimes we need to release the ideals we cling to and reimagine our lives. I don't know what tomorrow may bring. What I do know is, today, I am happy.

ABOUT THE AUTHOR

MJ Corkern is a writer, speaker and connecter and Tarot card reader. She's a bleeding heart empath hippy witch who loves big, laughs loud and has worked tirelessly to heal from the traumas evangelicalism and purity culture inflicted on her. She recently launched a coaching practice, using her experiences to help others heal from similar wounds. In her free time, MJ enjoys spending time with her family and catching up on her favorite shows.

MJ is me. I'm writing this bio myself. I created and published this work to help others heal from or perhaps better understand the kind of damage purity culture has done to women.

As an indie author, I do not have the power of a publishing house (or a marketing team) behind me and rely on word of mouth to help get this book into the hands of those who could benefit from it. If this book helped you or entertained you, please consider telling your friends, leaving a review on Amazon, and connecting with me on social media!

facebook.com/mjcorkernauthor

twitter.com/mjcorkern

instagram.com/mjcorkernauthor

ACKNOWLEDGMENTS

This book would not exist if it weren't for a few amazing people.

First and foremost, thank you Luis, for listening tirelessly to my doubts and fears, for offering me continued support, feedback and encouragement.

To Rose, my dream editor, thank you for all your hard work. You knew exactly what I was trying to say and would find a better, smoother way to phrase things. You have a gift, and I'm so thankful to have found you, which brings me to Stephanie.

Stephanie, thank you for introducing me to Rose, thank you for being my very first beta reader and a consistent cheer leader. Being on your Razed Evangelical podcast was a blast and I'm glad to call you a friend.

To my cousin Alaina, you have been a source of encouragement, and you too, helped improve this work. Thank you for reading it and offering feedback and for always being there for me.

Made in the USA
Monee, IL
30 October 2020